RIGHT HERE
WAITING

K.E. BELLEDONNE

interlude  press. • new york

Dedication:

To my Uncle Pete and his partner of 27 years, Randy— for showing me how lasting love can be.

And to a good friend, whose steadfast support and witty banter have sustained me through this entire process.

Back when this story was just spark in my head, I had a conversation with my friend about the Golden Age of Hollywood movies we adored and grew up on. And he made a passing comment about feeling, growing up a gay man, that those stories weren't really for him, about how he'd feared he wouldn't ever get a happy ending, because all the happy endings in those books and movies weren't about "people like him," as he put it.

I set out to change that, as best I could.

A wildly romantic story, full of action, adventure, mildly implausible plot-points and earnest declarations of love, just like those old movies we love; where the action and drama come from the situations they find themselves in, not because of who they love. I hope you can hear the violin soundtrack in the background, the title cards sweeping across the screen, just like in the movies…

Lex, my friend, my secret is out. This was all written just for you.

PROLOGUE

Benjamin Williams always hated being alone on Christmas Eve.

He'd kept busy all day, delivering presents to his nearby friends, though with the snowstorm coming, he'd made sure to be home early. The bumpers on their Packard had long since been sacrificed to the scrap metal drive; the tires were worn nearly bald and they wouldn't be getting new ones—not when "Our Boys Over There" needed every shred of rubber for the war effort.

Ben always capitalized Our Boys Over There in his head whenever he said it, whenever he heard it. It really translated to "Peter." Everything he did, every drive he participated in, every War Bond he bought, every vegetable he planted, every hour of every extra shift he picked up at the factory, every extra thing he could do despite the trick knee that barred him from enlisting, was for Pete. To help Pete. To help Pete so much that the Air Forces wouldn't need him anymore and would send him home. To help the war effort so greatly that it'd be over tomorrow and Pete would be here, safe in his arms, the next time Ben woke up.

He woke from dreams sobbing into the night, reaching out for Pete. Dreams in which Pete arrived unannounced on their doorstep, dreams of meeting his train at the station and running through the mist to meet him, dreams of being surprised by Pete casually swinging around the corner of the house at one of their friends' backyard parties.

He stepped into their kitchen—so efficient, so modern—and opened a fresh jar of strawberry preserves, made from the patch he'd carefully tended in the victory garden that had been their backyard. Pete had always hated to mow, anyway, so Ben hadn't hesitated to plow up the lawn to plant vegetables, potatoes, carrots, beans—anything to augment his own pantry, so he could donate more to the war effort. The small patch of strawberries hiding in the corner had thrived; Pete would often slip out on summer mornings, barefoot into the dew, to pick a handful of strawberries to share with Ben over breakfast. And he'd left the rosebushes that had been planted by the previous owners. They tangled over and through the fence in the defiant, determined way that roses have, managing to survive, even thrive, once their roots have taken hold, no matter what happens to them.

Ben spread strawberry preserves on toasted bread, grabbed two cookies he'd saved from the batches he'd made for his family back home—using up his entire month's sugar ration—a cup of Earl Grey tea, no lemon, and walked back to the living room. He glanced around the room. Two leather club chairs faced each other, snug near the lit stone fireplace. The staircase banister was twined with dark green garland. A Christmas tree, brightly colored glass balls gleaming, sat in the small bay window. A large radio in a wood case stood in the corner, the tubes warming already. He set his plate and cup with its saucer on the spindly table next to it. The table next to Pete's chair was decidedly more stable, more solid—Pete had a habit of knocking things over during exciting moments in radio programs.

The decorations this year were less exuberant than in years past. Just the tree, with its glass balls; a few of Ben's mother's porcelain angels on the mantel, nestled in evergreen garland; and some candles, still waiting to be lit. Ben had started a fire in the fireplace. It was now a lovely little fire, popping and crackling. A sprig of mistletoe was hung cheekily from the reading lamp—it had always made Pete smile.

Ben added another log to the fire, shivering slightly as he looked out the window at the snow still falling. He plumped the pillows in his chair. He'd left Pete's pillows crushed just the way he'd left them. When Pete came home, he could sit in his chair and wouldn't have to fuss at all.

He turned the dial to find the special Christmas Eve program broadcast from locations all around the world so Our Boys Over There could hear sounds from home, and so their families—praying, hoping, wishing and patiently and steadfastly waiting for them—could hear their soldier's voices.

He listened to a big band broadcasting from what could only be New York City; a short comedy skit Ben thought must be from Hollywood; a tiny band broadcasting from somewhere secret—from the accent of the singer, he guessed Scotland; another comedy sketch by soldiers somewhere in the Pacific; and then a scratchy reading of a poem from "somewhere in Europe."

After a short pause, the announcer spoke: "And now, coming to you from a secret location, pre-recorded earlier today, in cooperation with the Armed Forces Radio Network, we are proud to present one of our brave young men, United States Army Air Forces Captain Peter Montgomery, performing a special song from all our troops here to all of you folks back home."

Ben gasped and rushed to the radio to turn up the volume. He closed his eyes and pictured Pete standing in front of the microphone in his freshly pressed uniform—khaki, the color of his eyes when he laughed— standing surefooted and strong. Crowds never made Pete nervous; singing for millions of people over the radio wouldn't be a problem for him. When they'd sung duets during Ben's shows at the Black Cat supper club, Pete was always so smooth and sure, never a tremor or nerves. And now, Ben could just picture him: Pete's eyes would be closed; he'd have a slight smile; his hands would be either gently folded behind his back or holding the microphone stand.

The honey sound of Pete's voice singing "I'll Be Home for Christmas"—a voice Ben hadn't heard in so long—poured from the radio, simple and unaccompanied. He sank to his knees in front of the set and turned the volume even louder. He reached out with one finger to caress the wood, stained golden-red because Pete swore it was the same color as Ben's hair in the summer. The set reverberated under his fingers. Ben put his entire hand on the set, feeling the vibrations of Pete's voice through the wood in almost the same way as he'd felt Pete's voice through his chest when Pete would sing him to sleep, Pete's naked chest under Ben's palm, their legs tangled and bodies satiated.

Ben didn't feel the tears streaming down his face and ignored the pain in his knee as he knelt there—he only felt Pete. Pete's happiness and joy in the world, Pete's kindness and generosity, Pete's caring and love—Ben was enveloped in thoughts of Pete. For this short song, a song of longing and dreams of home, which he knew Pete had picked just for them, he and Pete were together, just as they'd be together again, someday soon.

After the song ended, Ben heard Pete whisper, "Merry Christmas."

"Merry Christmas," Ben whispered back. "Be safe, darling. Come home soon."

CHAPTER ONE

THEY HAD GONE TO THE recruitment office separately. First, Ben, before lunch. Then Pete, after lunch. They didn't want to raise any eyebrows.

No one in New York City so much as batted their eyelashes at two bachelors sharing an apartment, not with the steady stream of women in and out of there. The girls who lived downstairs, Bets McCaffrey and Ginger O'Reilly, frequently stayed the night, according to the neighbors. The lady in 11A was sure Bets was Benjamin's girlfriend and Ginger was Peter's; the man in 11C was sure Bets was Pete's girl and Ginger was Ben's; the ladies in 11D didn't care to speculate, lest it provoke inquiries into their own living arrangement.

Ben and Pete meticulously kept up the appearance, decorating both bedrooms, though "Peter's room" was clearly the repository for anything that was too sentimental to throw away and didn't match the décor of the rest of their bachelor pad. Ben was busy with his tailor shop, Pete with managing part of his family's stock market fund on Wall Street.

They were to meet at the apartment to share their news. Pete burst through the door promptly at six to the smell of Ben cooking.

Pete grabbed him from behind, wrapping his arms tightly around Ben's waist, peering down over Ben's shoulder at the pots being stirred. They were both tall, though Pete, to his chagrin, was the shorter of the two. Pete was rawboned and lanky, Ben was firmly muscled. They barely fit in the tiny apartment kitchen at the same time.

"Hello, handsome," he purred in Ben's ear.

"Hello, you." Ben pressed the side of his head against Pete's. "Dinner's just about ready. Would you get the plates ready?"

Pete grabbed the plates and silverware from the sideboard and twisted fresh napkins into their monogrammed napkin rings. He poured a sizable measure of whiskey into cut-glass highball glasses, splashed in some water and met Ben, who was coming from the kitchen laden with serving dishes. After they had dropped their napkins in their laps, Pete picked up his whiskey and raised it in a toast.

"Here's to new adventures. I report for training in two weeks! And you?" he smiled expectantly.

Ben, his own glass raised, faltered. "I… they… they said my knee is not strong enough. I… I didn't make it."

Pete had had the idea of enlisting in the first place, Pete who believed in kindness and decency and freedom and wholesomeness. Ben was more cynical, inclined to wait. *Pete, they won't want* us *anyway.*

But the strength of Pete's convictions had worked on him. With newsreels and newspapers, reports and stories about the dangers of war, the steady propaganda appealing to his heart, Ben finally decided to enlist as well. He couldn't bear the thought of staying behind while Pete marched into danger. He knew there was little to no chance of them being stationed together. But he had a romantic notion that they would find each other in an Officer's Club somewhere in Europe, or he would jump into a trench and there would be Pete.

Ben wasn't sure how he was going to live through being left behind, stand and watch Pete board a train and not know when—or if, oh God, *or if*—he'd see him again. Was he strong enough? Could he bear not having Pete near him?

Dinner was subdued. They spoke of Ben's father's health, the recent visit of Pete's brother, a new project at work. No talk of war or danger or leaving.

Yet later, Ben turned to Pete in bed and fiercely and silently made love to him, knowing Pete understood. Ben would always, always, be right here waiting for him, no matter what the cost.

* * *

THEY WERE KEPT BUSY ASSEMBLING things Pete would be allowed to bring to flight school, beyond what the Army would supply, and phoning their parents to tell them the news; the two weeks before Pete had to report for training flew by. Bets and Ginger threw a cocktail party. Alice and Johnny came over to bake cookies.

Tom and Tony took them out to dinner one night—Ben got horribly drunk. When they got home, Pete had to help him vomit into the toilet, holding him tightly on the cold tiles of their bathroom floor, whispering words of love and comfort into his hair.

And then it was the last weekend.

On Friday, they tossed their suitcases in the backseat of their car and hit the road, headed for their bungalow. They stopped at the small grocery on the edge of their little beach town for supplies: wine, bread, cheese, fruit, and a large cured sausage Pete waved at Ben, suggestively waggling his eyebrows.

Ben unlocked the heavy front door and motioned for Pete to enter first, which he did after bowing with a ridiculous flourish. The front door opened onto a steep staircase to the small loft; downstairs, a single large room with a massive rough stone fireplace served as parlor and dining room. On the mantle, a vase full of sea glass they'd collected together caught the morning light and glowed. Ben immediately laid and lit a fire to drive out the lingering damp, while Pete went around the tiny house, stripping off the dust sheets, opening the windows to let in fresh air.

They unpacked their groceries from the crackling paper sacks, putting things away carefully in the tiny cupboards. The kitchen was at the back of the house, with large windows facing the beach. Space was at a premium; bookshelves lined every wall, overflowing with books and photos and knickknacks and the collection of stones they had picked up in their wanderings—stones that were beautiful in some way, or just felt good in their hands. Pete always kept his eye out for rocks shaped like hearts to bring to Ben.

They were far enough from town that no one just dropped by, and any visitors they had were friends who already knew about them. The neighbors they had met were polite, but incurious. The bungalow was far down the beach, away from all the others, and they relished their privacy. No need to pretend they were anything other than themselves, here.

This house only had one bedroom. When they took their bags up to their room, Ben dropped them roughly just inside the door.

"Don't even bother opening those," Ben smiled wickedly.

Shoving him back against the wall, Ben roughly unknotted Pete's tie. He knelt in front of him, unzipped his trousers and, taking Pete into his mouth, explained without words his plan for the weekend.

MUCH LATER, THEY SPENT TIME puttering around the house, as though it was just a normal weekend for them. Ben replaced the burned-out light bulb in the hall closet. Pete stood on the stepladder and dusted the ceiling fan. Ben brought in armfuls of wood and put them in the bin near the fireplace. Pete sharpened the blades of the old push mower and mowed the tiny lawn.

Afterward, he collapsed in the hammock and when Ben brought him a glass of fresh lemonade, Pete pulled him down into the hammock beside him—nearly tipping them both out—and kissed him until neither of them could see straight.

Just a normal weekend. Except that it wasn't.

* * *

MONDAY MORNING, BEN TOOK PETE to the train station.

They'd said their farewells already, in the privacy of the apartment, in the dark of their bed, in the sunshine of their kitchen. Kisses and touches, while Ben made coffee and Pete made toast in their tiny kitchen, slipping around each other with caressing hands and bodies. They sat at their table with coffee they barely sipped and toast neither of them tasted.

"You know, P, I'm afraid I'm going to go crazy around here without you," Ben said quietly, his coffee cup clattering against its saucer as he set it down. He'd been trying to hold it in, trying to keep his disappointment from darkening the time they had left together. It wasn't Pete's fault, after all. But he just couldn't keep it in any longer. "I... I don't want to just sit around here as if I'm the girl he left behind—"

"For one thing," Pete interrupted, one eyebrow raised rakishly, "I consider myself an expert on your body and I can assure you, you are not a girl. You are most definitely a man. I would know."

"Oh, would you, now?" Ben snorted lightly, toying with the edge of his place mat.

"And as for being 'left behind,'" Pete continued, "I'm coming back. So if you're picturing being Lillian Crosby in that movie where What's-His-Name flies off to Cairo and gets cursed by the mummy, and she gets left behind at the airport in Chicago in the fog wearing the fabulous hat and veil, you've got another thing coming."

Ben couldn't quite manage the laugh he knew Pete was trying to get from him.

"I just don't want to be useless. I know… I know people are already going to be suspicious of me—why haven't I volunteered; what's wrong with me; why am I shirking? I just don't want to sit around and do *nothing*. I'll go crazy."

"Ginger is going to need help keeping Bets in line—"

"Oh, what fun…" Ben shook his head. "My knee hasn't been a problem for *years* now. I barely even notice it anymore."

"For which I am grateful. But, B, you've got the shop to keep you busy and singing at the Black Cat… and someone's got to keep an eye on Bets."

"Oh God, that's true. All these soldiers on leave here in the city. I might have to lock her in her closet."

"I'll be home again before you know it. It'll fly by."

Ben bit his lip and nodded, smiling as brightly as he could manage. "I'll find something to do, I'm sure. Don't you worry about me."

"I *will* worry about you. It's my job to worry about you."

"I'll worry about you, too."

"Thank you, baby."

JUST INSIDE THEIR FRONT DOOR, Pete wrapped his arms around Ben's waist, pressed his forehead to Ben's forehead. "It's not goodbye. It's 'See you later.' I'm coming back. I am coming back."

Ben tried to manage a watery smile. He sniffed. "Right. See you later." He grabbed Pete's fedora from the hat stand and set it on his hair.

Pete wiped the tear trailing down his lover's cheek. "It's a couple of months. And I'll be an officer! You've always had a thing for men in uniform," Pete tried to tease.

Ben sniffed again.

"Hey. I promise. I'm coming back."

"You better. I love you"

"I love you, too, baby. So much."

But here, on the train platform, there was nothing they could say, nowhere they could touch. With a smile that wouldn't quite stay firm, a wink and a jaunty salute, Pete hoisted his bag to his shoulder and stepped up into the train car.

Ben put his arms behind his back, twisting his fingers until they went numb. He smiled widely, a smile that didn't reach his eyes.

The conductor blew his whistle. Last minute passengers hurried to board. Ben saw Pete walking down the aisle, looking for an empty seat. Ben followed him down the platform, standing well back from the edge of the track. He leaned against a pillar, watching Pete get his bag up on the rack. He could see Pete's dark brows knit in concentration and distress as he settled himself in the seat next to the window.

The whistle blew again. Puffs of steam rose, fogging Ben's view. He welcomed it. Maybe no one would notice the tears he could no longer keep inside.

If the men sitting across from Pete noticed the sheer panic that flashed in his eyes when the train lurched on its way, or the way his hand slammed the glass as if he was reaching for someone outside, they didn't say a word.

* * *

BEN RETURNED TO THE APARTMENT to find Bets and Ginger standing in front of their door. Ben smiled brightly, and sighed—a sigh and a smile that crumbled when Ginger held out her arms to him. Bets took his key ring from him—Pete had bought matching silver fobs engraved with their monograms—and unlocked the door. After picking up paper bags laden with groceries, she pushed Ben and Ginger through the door, and, before the rest of the apartment dwellers could hear the sobs tearing from his throat, kicked it shut behind them.

After Ben got himself back under control—still not able to escape a few sniffs and a nagging hitch in his breath—Bets doled out the cheesecake, while Ginger made them a fresh pot of coffee.

Bets, a department store model, and Ginger, a nurse at the hospital, came part and parcel, a package deal. They'd met the two girls when Ginger had come flying upstairs one afternoon, enraged at the hammering going on and on and on and bent on venting her frustration on whichever neighbor was perpetrating it. When she saw it was Pete performing an impromptu tap routine, she lost most of the wind in her sails. When Bets came home four hours later and was also annoyed by the noise, she had found Ginger and Pete working their way through a dance routine from *Top Hat,* the carpets in the living room rolled up, and Ben lying on the couch, howling with laughter and encouragement. The four of them had been inseparable ever since.

"Coffee's the ticket, ducks. Perk us right up and we'll be good as new." Ginger struggled to tame a strand of her reddish orange hair as she took in Ben's swollen, red eyes looking up at her. "Well, almost, I guess."

"Coffee, cheesecake," Bets prescribed as she handed Ben a slice of dessert on plate. "And some cold compresses for the eyes."

Her blond hair glistened in the sunlight as she stood and briskly walked to the kitchen.

"Benny, do you have any cucumber?" she called.

"Bottom shelf of the icebox." Ben's voice was hoarse. He cleared his throat. "If we have any left, I suppose."

Both girls returned from the kitchen—Ginger with a steaming pot of coffee, Bets with a cold wet washcloth and three forks.

"We'll do the cucumber compresses later. For now, let's dig into this cheesecake and drink that coffee before it gets cold!" Bets grinned, folding her tiny body into the armchair near the fireplace.

He smiled back. It wasn't a big smile and it wasn't for very long, but it was a real one. He lay back against the couch, rested his head on the arm and carefully dropped the cloth over his eyes.

"Honey, you know he's okay, right? He's in training; it'll be rough, but it'll be over quick and he'll be back." Ginger plopped onto the couch next to him. Always filled with exuberance, Ginger had all the well-meaning grace of a baby giraffe.

"He'll be back in nine months, for two weeks. And then he'll be sent overseas, into death and destruction and filth and misery and foxholes and bombs and I can't—I can't—" The cloth dropped from Ben's panicked eyes.

"Whoa, whoa, whoa, there, cowboy," Ginger gently tugged on Ben's hand, pulling it away from his mouth, looking into his eyes intently. "Breathe. We'll worry about that bridge when we get to it. For now, Pete is safe. He's safe, do you hear me? There's no need to fall apart."

Ben looked down at the pillow in his lap, tracing the pattern with a gentle fingertip, lips trembling. "If he's still not here in three days, it'll be the longest we've been apart since the day we met."

* * *

IT HAD BEEN ONE OF those brilliantly sunny, deathly cold early mornings in the city. Ben was headed home from his tailor shop, head bent, nose running, hands stuffed in his pockets, his shoulders hunched against the wind that threatened to rip his scarf from his neck as he skirted the tall wrought-iron fence of Gramercy Park.

He remembered seeing a pair of dog eyes, then two pairs, remembered the two golden retrievers grinning up at him before darting away, a sharp tug on his ankles, then something heavy landed on him as the sky swirled above him.

"Oh, blast! Oh, hey, are you okay?" Anxious eyes had peered into his—eyes the color of honey—above a similarly anxious mouth.

"Ooof." Ben was breathless, and not just from the fall. The owner of those warm eyes was lying on top of him in the middle of the park path. With the tight feeling around his legs and the excited yipping of the dogs, he surmised they'd both been tangled in the dogs' leashes. An impressive feat of strength for the dogs, sweeping two grown men right off their feet.

Ben nodded, swallowing hard at the feeling of the stranger's body crushed against his. The man planted his hands on either side of Ben's head and levered up his torso. A better view of his face, for Ben, but jeepers if it wasn't grinding his hips down into Ben's... unmentionables. Ben swallowed again. The stranger kicked his legs and muttered as he untangled them from the dogs.

"Gosh, I am so sorry. Are you all right?" Those brown eyes were warm and melting and, as the stranger took Ben's hand to pull him up, Ben was pretty sure he was going to swoon.

"I'm... Yeah, I'm fine," Ben finally managed, blushing. They were about the same height, both broad-shouldered and tall. Ben, with a tailor's eye, thought the man could use a differently cut coat. Though the wool was soft to the touch and obviously of good quality, the shape did nothing to flatter his lanky frame.

"Oh no, look at your pants. Oh gosh, I'm so sorry." Ben looked down in surprise—he hadn't noticed the muddy slush seeping into the seat of his trousers. The stranger still held Ben's hand.

"Listen, let me get rid of these dogs—I'm just walking them for a friend—and then let me buy you a cup of coffee at this little place around the corner. Or you could come back to my— you just can't go walking around in pants like that."

"I'd—okay." Ben could feel a dopey smile on his face. He cleared his throat. "I'd— I'd like that."

"Umm, I'm Pete. Peter Montgomery." Pete smiled. Ben's knees felt wobbly.

He smiled back, stammering, "Benjamin. Benjamin Williams."

Pete whistled and the dogs came to heel. He gathered up their leashes, carefully locked the park gate and slipped the key into his pocket. He took Ben's elbow in his palm and steered them toward the tall, stately brick apartment building just across the street.

"It's good of you to walk those dogs, Mr. Montgomery." The doorman smiled as he opened the large plate glass doors for them. "Mr. Johnson could never manage it now."

Pete smiled in return. "Just being neighborly, Thomas."

They waited for the elevator, the dogs miraculously sitting patiently at their feet. Ben watched the large brass needle trace its arc down until it reached the ground floor.

Pete ushered Ben into the elevator, stepped in beside him and clicked his tongue at the dogs, who once again came to sit at their feet. He pressed eleven, and they rode in silence, each of them pretending not to glance at the other and blushing when they got caught.

At 11C, Pete rang the doorbell. An old man opened the door.

"Oh, Peter, my boy. Thank you so much for doing this."

"No problem, Mr. Johnson, no problem at all. Same time tomorrow?" Pete smiled warmly.

"That would be wonderful, Peter, if it's not too much trouble for you." Mr. Johnson looked feeble, tired, but happy.

"Of course, Mr. Johnson." Pete turned and directed Ben down the hall. Mr. Johnson shut the door behind them.

At 11B, Pete unlocked the door and ushered Ben inside.

"I... um. I think I might have a change of clothes you could borrow, if you... if you want." Pete looked suddenly nervous, darting his eyes around his apartment, looking at anything but Ben.

Ben seemed to have something stuck in throat. "Oh, no, I don't want to be any trouble. I—"

"Ohhh, no, no. It's no trouble at all. It's just... your pants are a bit—"

Pete nodded his chin at Ben's legs. Ben suddenly realized that the front of his pants were, in fact, soaked—and were clinging to him in a most decidedly indecent manner.

Pete flushed, nodded awkwardly, then darted down the hall. Ben wasn't sure if he should follow him, or stay where he was or... *no, definitely don't follow him, Ben, he's probably going to his bedroom and you do NOT need to be in his bedroom wearing soaking wet pants. No, Ben.*

Pete returned, shaking out a pair of navy gabardine trousers. "I think these will fit. The, ummm, the bath is just here." He motioned toward a door just down the hall.

Ben took the trousers. Their fingertips brushed, and an electric shock—an actual spark—flew between them.

They both gasped and laughed.

"Thank you. I'll be right out. And then, I believe you promised coffee?" Ben smiled.

Pete's answering smile lit up the entire room. *Maybe even the entire world*, Ben thought as his heart soared.

"Yes, Ben. I do believe I did."

They almost left for the coffee shop exactly seven times that day. Instead, they sat on Pete's couch, primly at first, but growing ever closer to each other as they laughed and talked and giggled and swapped stories and told jokes, and neither one of them could—or would—deny the bubble of happiness in their chests.

By their seventh attempt, Pete had made three pots of coffee, four sandwiches and several gin and tonics. They sat in the middle of the couch, facing each other, knees touching. As Ben reached a particularly exciting part in the story he was telling—trapped in an elevator at Bergdorf's with a Vanderbilt cousin and her hyperactive Pomeranian—he reached out and grabbed Pete's forearm.

Pete couldn't stop staring at Ben's hand on his arm. Ben's mouth felt dry as Pete's hand moved slowly to cover Ben's own.

This was a moment. A moment they both knew could go very, very wrong, very, very quickly.

Ben's voice drifted into silence, as Pete's fingertip slowly traced the delicate veins and tendons in Ben's hand. He lifted his eyes to meet Ben's. His face was flushed and expectant; his lips parted slightly. Neither of them seemed able to breathe steadily.

"Ben?" Pete's voice was soft and quiet and unexpectedly vulnerable.

Ben took a deep breath and surged forward, fitting his mouth to Pete's as if he'd always been a part of him.

When their lips finally parted, rosy and joyful, their eyes were shining. The subtle tension—not altogether unpleasant, but tension nonetheless—had been released.

"I was so afraid that you weren't—weren't —" Pete shook his head, trying to clear it, still toying with Ben's hand. "That you weren't—*like me.*"

Ben's smile broke into a wide grin. "But I am. I am *like you* and I *do* like you."

Pete sighed happily and ran his fingers through the hair above Ben's ear, dragging them back around under his jaw, to kiss him again.

When they broke apart, no longer bashful, flushed and panting and still joyful but also desperately needing, Pete sat back to try to catch his breath.

"We should—we should go get dinner."

Ben was dizzy with the happiness; heat raced through his veins. His heart was pounding; his head was spinning. He was sure it was only the look in Pete's eyes that kept him from floating away.

Pete chuckled and somehow tore himself away from Ben sitting there on his couch—gorgeous, handsome, right here, so close, and so beautiful—stood and walked to look out the window at the dark night sky. "I think it's snowing," he said, wrinkling his nose.

"Oh goody." Ben giggled.

"Goody?" Pete teased. He vaulted over the back of the couch, landing against the seat with a bounce that so helpfully propelled Ben into his arms.

"Could I eat here?" Ben folded his arms across Pete's chest, resting his chin on them.

"Uhhhhh. Yes? I think so?" Pete smiled down at Ben, trying to remember what might be in his kitchen. "I think I have some roast beef from last night; we could make some potatoes—"

Ben dropped his voice to a low purr, his eyelashes dropping demurely against his cheeks. "That's not quite what I was talking about."

Pete let out a loud huff of laughter.

"Let me loosen your tie, Mr. Williams, if I may." Pete's diction was precise and formal, but the searing look in his eyes made Ben's breathing stutter.

"Oh, please do, Mr. Montgomery."

* * *

BEN CLEARED HIS THROAT—GINGER HAD never heard the story of how he and Pete had met—and continued.

"And then, after he said it was snowing, we… then we had some cold roast beef with scalloped potatoes—our first time cooking together—and we listened to the radio." *While I fucked him over the back of his couch.* "And then the storm was so wild, he insisted I stay the night." *And then we fucked in the kitchen, on the dining room table, on the bathroom floor because the logistics of the bathtub were too daunting; and by the time we made it to the bedroom, the storm had been over for three days, and we were making love.*

CHAPTER TWO

Ben nearly snatched the letter from the doorman, addressed to "B. Williams" in Pete's bold handwriting. He started to rip the envelope on his way to the elevator. Not wanting to tear the letter inside, his first word from Pete in two weeks, he calmed himself until he got safely inside the apartment and went in search of the letter opener—a miniature brass sword that Pete always pretended was a broadsword whenever he opened the mail.

Dear B—

I'm writing to you from just outside S—— About all I can say is it's hot and dusty and I miss you more than I can possibly tell you.

Flight training looks like it will be interesting, if the textbooks they've given us are any indication. The physical tests started right after the bus dropped us off from the train station. They weren't as difficult as I'd feared. I passed them easily—much easier than several of the guys.

My room is small, just four bunk beds, a desk and a chair. I share it with Jim Livingston, a Texas boy, Charlie Thompson, from Maine and Bill Livingston, from Chicago. They are all friendly. Charlie and I got the short straw (and, oh God, I sincerely hope you've just raised your eyebrow and are about to make one of your usual jokes about my height, because that's how I'm imagining you and, oh God, you're beautiful)—so he and I are on the top bunks. There is sand and dust everywhere.

The barracks are cinder block—unattractive and depressing, but at least they hold the cool longer. By the time it was lights-out last night, it was swelteringly hot and I couldn't sleep, which probably accounts for my dark mood right now.

I'm sorry, sweetheart, for writing to you while I'm feeling blue. I'm tired from the train trip, tired from the tests and the exams. I promise, everything's fine. I'll get a good night's rest tonight (because I can hear in my head that that's what you're saying I need) and dream of you, and tomorrow, it'll be better.

I hope this letter reaches you in one piece. Rumor has it the censors here can be a little overzealous at times.

I love you, darling, so very, very much. I'm here, I'm fine, everything's going to be all right. This time is going to fly by—pun intended. I'm here, doing important work that will help make the world a better place. Everything's going to be okay.

All my love, always.

Your P—

He sat at the desk in the living room and stared at the snapshot of Pete laughing on the beach last summer that was tucked into the frame of a more formal studio portrait from his college graduation.

My darling P—

I'm writing to you from the desk in our apartment. It's cool and dark here. It's been raining since you left. I think the sun misses competing with your smiles.

The censors did take out your location— but it doesn't really matter where you are. All I know is you're not Here.

Bets and Ginger send their love. They've been coming over every day, with the most pathetic excuses—oh, I thought I left my hairbrush here; oh, can I borrow that book? I know they're checking up on me, which I secretly appreciate and am outwardly annoyed at—but I know you'd want to know that I'm not alone.

Work is going well. I'm still doing one show a week at the Black Cat. I'm going to piece together a quilt for our bed. Ginger wants me to teach her how to knit, but I'm honestly afraid. I hope you're laughing at the

picture in your head of Ginger absolutely tangled head-to-toe in a skein of
yarn, wailing while sitting on the floor and then bursting into that loud,
obnoxious and entirely wonderful laugh of hers. You know as well as I do
that's exactly how it's going to go.

Tell me more about school, if you can. What are your roommates like?

I'm glad you're well and I'm happy to hear things look interesting to
you. Don't forget to drink your water; dehydration is a dangerous thing.
Plus, it always makes you cranky.

I love you, P, I love you I love you I love you.

Yours always.

Me

He spritzed the sheets of light blue paper with a bottle of Bets's perfume
she'd left at their apartment, just for fun. He knew Pete would recognize
it, knew it'd make him chuckle. He carefully copied the address onto the
envelope and placed it on the hall table near the door. He'd mail it after
lunch.

* * *

A BRIEF LETTER ARRIVED FOR Ben the next week. He could almost hear
what Pete was really saying.

Dear B—

It was so lovely to receive your letter and get a whiff of home. I know
you know how I miss that scent. I know Bets is driving you nuts, and the
smell of her perfume is probably already setting your teeth on edge, but
she's trying to take care of you now that I can't. Please let her.

My roommates are swell. I have only chatted with them briefly and
am keeping them at arm's length for now, but, so far, have discovered
nothing upsetting about them. *School is incredibly interesting; I'm really*
happy I chose the Air Forces. You know how I've always dreamed of
being able to fly and Ben, it's incredible beautiful wonderful and nearly
everything I ever thought it would be, even if it's in a loud metal tube

instead of with bird's wings. *The work is tough, but they've already taken us up on our first few flights.* I cried the first time I piloted the plane and realized I was flying—FLYING, Ben. It was freedom and joy and the only thing that could convince me to land again was the thought of you.

I promise, I am staying hydrated. They're feeding us quite well, though there's no midnight snack. Like I usually bring back to bed and eat off your stomach and you pretend to yell at me for getting crumbs all over you but then you don't complain at all when I lick them up. *We get our first liberty this weekend, and Jim says he's going to take us to an incredible barbecue place. I hope it's everything he says it is.* And not a whorehouse as well, because, oh God Benny, that's going to be awkward. Stop laughing, you bastard, it's not going to be funny. It's going to be downright awkward.

The physical training has been fine—not too difficult for me, particularly the upper body strength testing. Which you know I aced because I lift weights because I know what the sight of my chest does to you, and I very much like that response.

I'll write you again as soon as I can. We have our first exams coming up and I'm determined to ace them all.

I love you, darling. Be well. I hope you're going out and having fun with The Girls. Please let them take you out and make you smile. I can't bear the thought of you not smiling.

All my love, always.

P.

* * *

THE TRIP TO THE BARBECUE place turned out to be exactly as Pete feared—a restaurant-slash-cathouse on the outskirts of town. The food was, in fact, excellent—Pete couldn't deny that. Barbecued brisket that melted in your mouth, baked beans like he'd never tasted before, roasted corn on the cob, and by the time the meal was over, he'd been certain he'd never be able to move again.

And that's when the girls arrived.

Before he knew it, they were surrounded by a crowd of women, scantily clad, flirtatious and smiling and dripping with perfume. Jim's steady gray eyes lit up. Charlie swiped the blond shock of hair that always fell in his eyes and looked bashful. Bill, his grin flashing, was already pulling one of the girls into his lap. Pete wasn't quite sure what to do.

The girls were circling—*like vultures over a dead ox*—trying to decide who might be potential customers. One of them sat down next to him and put her hand on his arm. He smiled but shook his head.

"Sorry. Not interested."

"Oh now, sugar. Don't be like that." Her eyes were the faint blue of denim coveralls washed too often, and shadowed with harsh color. Her eyelashes stirred something in him: the same dark brown as Ben's and just as entangled as Ben's blinking sleepily in their bed. But her hair was bleached blonde, not the melting red-gold of Ben's. Her skin was painted creamy white, not the cool gleam of Ben's.

He wanted Ben. This was the longest they'd ever been apart, and he felt wrong all over without him. He was desperate for him, thirsting for him, and all this girl right now reminded him of was what he could not have. She was small and wiry, with fine bones like a bird, while Ben was tall and lissome. She had nothing of Ben's strength, Ben's grace, Ben's—anything.

"And you're distinctly lacking some fairly specific physical attributes, besides—" He choked back the thought, coughing into his beer. Perhaps the beer was stronger than he'd thought.

Charlie switched seats, thumping down abruptly at his side. He folded his gangly legs neatly beneath the bench. "You heard the man, honey. You're wasting your time. And no. Don't look at me either. We've both got sweethearts back home who'll take a big ole knife to our nether regions if we get caught with our pants down with someone else. So, just move along."

She pouted for just a second, just to test if maybe he'd change his mind, if maybe he was just joking. But his face stayed serious, and she moved off in search of someone more welcoming.

Charlie nearly knocked over his glass of beer reaching for it and dragged it across the table. "So, Montgomery. You're married, right?"

Pete sipped at his drink slowly, considering his response.

"Might as well be," he offered.

"Yeah. Me, too. Met her in kindergarten and never had any reason to look at any other girl."

"That's sweet." Pete smiled.

"Yeah, she's a great girl. I want to get married when I get back from training, but she's not sure. She's known me twenty years, isn't sure if I'm husband-material. But, what can you do, you know?"

Pete chuckled, sipping his beer.

"What about you two? You been together long?"

"Yep." He thought he really should have had more practice with this, talking about Ben without *talking* about him. "A couple of years now."

"And you're not married yet?"

"Nah. Not yet."

"Maybe someday?" Charlie pressed.

"Perhaps." Pete grinned. "I'd like to."

"That's good. She still live with her parents?"

"Uhhhh. No." Pete hesitated, but Charlie seemed open-minded enough to hear this. "We... uhh... We live together."

"Oh man, that's great. You've got it made. No parents to get in the way, no one hanging over the back of the couch when you're trying to canoodle. That's great." He clapped Pete on the shoulder.

"Yeah. It's... great. It really is."

"Then you and me'll stick together. These guys—" he waved his beer bottle at the rest of the table, all in various states of seduction with the ladies of the establishment.

"They can wave their dicks around at anything with some lipstick and a pulse. You and me, we'll be good boys with our dicks in our pants and go home and marry our—" He belched quietly into his fist. "Par'n me."

"Our sweethearts."

"Exactly." Charlie raised his beer bottle and clinked the neck with Pete's.

"Cheers." Pete finished his beer, waving the bottle at the barkeep for another.

"You and me, Pete," Charlie crowed. "You and me.

* * *

BEN'S DEBUT AT THE BLACK Cat had been pure happenstance. He'd stopped in front of it on his way home one evening, struggling against his umbrella in a real gale of a rainstorm, when he'd heard the unmistakable trumpet wail beginning "Stormy Weather." The appropriateness of the song to the situation at hand had made him laugh, so he'd gone in, to get out of the pelting rain, and maybe have a drink to warm up before he caught his death in the cold.

The club had been all but deserted on a Monday evening, the combo playing together for the fun of it rather than to impress the patrons. After two Manhattans and a Bellamy Scotch Sour, he'd found himself sitting at a table near the stage, eating a delicious dinner pressed upon him by a waitress who clucked at him and his dripping overcoat. Between bites, he had hummed along absentmindedly, losing himself in the warmth spreading outward from his belly, where the Scotch melted together with the baked potato and steak and left him feeling pleasantly calm and befuddled.

"Hey, you know '*Begin the Beguine?*'" the saxophone player had leaned forward to ask him. "Sing along with this next one."

And that's how had begun. At first, it had been just Monday nights, or every once in a while on Thursday, if he was passing by and had time. Once word had spread, and the club's popularity grew, the club owners had asked him to come back as a regular performer, and for years now he'd been performing every other Friday night. From time to time, he'd invite Pete up from the audience to sing a few tunes with him.

With Pete away at flight school, Ben didn't think his birthday seemed worth celebrating. After badgering and arguing, Bets and the boys in the band finally convinced him to celebrate at the Black Cat. Elaine, the waitress who'd fussed over him his first night there, brought him his favorite dinner and a bottle of champagne, on the house. The band had led the other diners in a rousing rendition of "Happy Birthday" while they brought out a cake covered in candles.

Ben had gone home soon after, stumbling a bit on the walk; he kissed Bets on the forehead as she got off the elevator at her floor and tripped on his way to his own front door. He drank a glass of water, splashed some on his face and sprawled face down on their bed. It didn't smell like Pete anymore.

He was no longer tired. Or maybe he was too tired. He couldn't decide, but he definitely decided he'd had too much to drink. With a disgruntled huff, he rolled onto his back and rubbed his eyes. This was so different from his last birthday, when Pete had insisted they stay in bed all day and brought him breakfast, lunch, birthday cake, afternoon tea and dinner, all in bed. They'd made love, napped, talked, listened to the radio, talked some more. They'd laughed and dreamed and planned.

He was just so *lonely* without Pete. He had friends and work and things to keep him busy, but without Pete to come home to, he felt lost.

At least this wasn't like the year they'd gone to celebrate Ben's birthday with his dad on the farm, back in Indiana. He hadn't been able to sleep that birthday, either. Though he and Pete had been together for quite a time, it was the first time his dad had met "his roommate," and he'd been a bundle of nerves the entire visit.

"I'm taking Pete to feed the calves, Dad," Ben had called as they walked out the kitchen door.

The barn was dimly lit, snug and close. Pete wrinkled his nose as the overwhelming smell of *cow* hit his nose in full force and Ben apologized ruefully.

"Yeah, I know. You get used it. Mostly."

The cows had been stalled with their calves, and lay placidly in their corners chewing their cuds while the calves wobbled and butted and were generally adorable. Pete just had to coo at them.

"You can pet them, if you want." Ben leaned over the gate, scratching the calf between her ears.

"She's not going to bite me?"

"Oh, you city boy." Ben shook his head. "Keep your fingers out of her mouth, and watch out for your buttons, because whatever they can get in their mouth, they will chomp down on. But no, she won't attack you. She's a cow, not a dog."

They watched them a while longer, then moved down the row to another stall. A calf, just a little older, was there all alone bawling loudly.

"Oh, you're a hungry guy, aren't you?" Ben grabbed a bottle full of milk from the dairy. Fitting a giant rubber nipple over the top, he'd handed it to Pete with a smile.

"What's this for?"

"Dad said he was born a few days ago, and was rejected by his mother. She refuses to let him nurse, so we've got to help him out until we can maybe get one of the other cows to take him."

"Ohhhhh, the poor little guy." Pete's forehead creased in sympathy. "You poor little thing."

The calf bleated loudly, already recognizing the bottle. He butted his head against the boards of the stall.

"Now, watch out, he's stronger than he looks," Ben cautioned as Pete leaned over the stall half-door with the bottle. The calf butted the stall again, making the boards rattle.

"I thought that might be the case," Ben said after watching a few moments.

"What? What's wrong?"

"He doesn't have the bottle thing figured out yet." Ben had insisted they change into coveralls, and now he was glad he did. "We're going to have to help him out."

He slipped open the lock on the stall door, pulling Pete inside as the calf rushed over to them.

"You're going to have to help him keep the nipple in his mouth. Watch your fingers."

Pete bent forward, offering the bottle, but the calf shied away.

"Hey, little guy. It's okay. You're okay," Pete cooed softly at the calf. "Aren't you hungry? I'm here with your dinner. Come on, little man."

The calf finally decided it was more hungry than skittish and latched on to the bottle fiercely. He tugged at it so hard, it slipped out of Pete's hands.

"Holy shit." Pete laughed, scrambling to catch the bottle as the calf tossed it. "He's a strong little one!"

"Just wait a few months. He'll mow you right over."

Pete regained control of the bottle, but the calf couldn't quite get the hang of keeping the bottle's nipple in his mouth. Listening to Pete babbling at the calf, trying to teach him tongue control had Ben nearly doubled over in laughter.

"Now just… that's right, just like… nooooo. Nope. Hang on. Try again." Pete had his mouth wide open, unconsciously mimicking the movements the calf was making. "There you go. Keep going—Oh, you lost it again. Hang on. Try again."

"Little one, this just is not working out." Pete shook his head gravely at the calf. "You're yanking my arms out of my sockets with all this pulling."

"And he's probably going to need a second bottle, too. You'll be all right in here by yourself while I go get it?"

"Oh, I think Sparky and I will be just fine."

"Sparky? His name is Sparky?"

"Yup," Pete beamed.

"Okay, well, you and Sparky sit pretty and I'll be right back with the rest of his dinner."

Ben returned from the dairy to find Pete sitting sprawled on the floor, the bottle hooked under his arm like a football and Sparky the calf sprawled across his legs.

"That's my good boy." With his free hand, Pete guided the recalcitrant nipple back into the calf's mouth, along with the calf's wayward tongue that couldn't quite coordinate its own efforts. There was hay in Pete's hair and a smudge of something Ben hoped was mud across his cheek, and he was sitting smack down in the muck and trampled hay of the stall. But the smile on Pete's face, radiant and magnificent and happy, made something swell in Ben's chest. He ducked into the stall, dropped to his knees next to Pete and pressed a quick kiss to a clean spot on his forehead.

"What's that for?" Pete laughed as the calf did his best to pull the nearly-empty bottle out of his arms.

"Couldn't help it."

Pete turned his head, craning his neck towards Ben. "Give me another."

Ben took advantage of this precious time alone, no family in the next room, no prying eyes, and kissed his love thoroughly.

"I love you, you know," Ben said quietly.

Pete glanced up, grinning brightly. "I love you, too."

"Let's get this guy bedded down for the night and go get cleaned up. Dinner will be ready soon." They forked out the dirty bedding as Sparky the calf romped around them before abruptly collapsing atop the fresh straw they'd spread and promptly falling asleep.

"Aw, look at the little guy." Pete stood behind Ben where he leaned on the pitchfork, wrapping his arms around Ben's waist and propping his chin on Ben's shoulder. "All tuckered out."

"It's hard work, being a calf."

Pete pressed his nose against Ben's neck and breathed him in, happy just for the moment to hold him close as Ben leaned back in his arms. They'd been at the farm for three days already, and Pete had just *missed* being close to him.

"I *love* you," he repeated.

"I love you, too."

"Oh," Ben's father's voice came from just behind them. They sprang apart as if they'd been burned, as they heard his footsteps quickly approaching.

"I didn't realize you two were out here," he said, glancing between the two of them before staring long and hard at the sleeping calf.

"Abby said the calves needed feeding, so I thought I'd show Pete how it's done."

"Good. Good." Ben's dad concentrated on the calf, tapping one fist lightly on the stall boards. "Well, Abigail's got dinner ready…"

"We'll go get washed up and get the table set," Pete offered quickly.

"No, I do believe she's got that settled," Ben's dad said gruffly. "You just get yourselves back to the house, washed up and ready to eat."

Ben kept his head down as they marched quickly back to the kitchen, climbed out of their coveralls and scrubbed their hands. Ben's father didn't warm up during dinner. Ben's sister Abby and Pete carried most of the conversation. Afterwards, while they helped Abby with the dishes, his dad sat in the parlor, listening to the radio.

Pete insisted on going to bed early—"and *alone*" he whispered, pushing Ben out the door of the guest bedroom, where he had been under the guise of making sure Pete had an extra blanket. Ben returned to the parlor, not quite sure what to expect—perhaps a lecture, perhaps an argument, but *something*. His dad finished his usual after-dinner pipe, flexing his feet in his worn slippers as they listened to the radio and went to bed without a word about it.

* * *

A WEEK LATER, ANOTHER LETTER from Pete arrived, and Ben bit his lip with worry, reading between the lines.

> *Dear B—*
>
> *I don't really know why I'm writing this to you right now—I don't want you to worry any further and I want you to believe I'm always safe and careful and there's nothing to be scared of. But nothing seems real until I share it with you. Not that I want this to be real, but I just can't get it through my head until I tell you.* Please, love, listen to me while I get all this out, otherwise I'm going to drown in it.
>
> *John MacPherson died today—he and his entire crew. He was one of my friends here, a real stand-up guy, kind and funny and a great dancer, and I don't know what to do about it. He and I ate breakfast together this morning. We were supposed to play pool tonight, against Bill and Tom. And now he's dead.* And I am feeling cold and numb and I need to curl up in your arms and have you tell me you're safe and I'm safe and everything will be okay, somehow.
>
> *He was out on a training flight—it was the same flight we did yesterday and there shouldn't have been anything that could have gone wrong. But it did. We—Charlie and Jim and I—were at the airfield, playing ball with some of the other crews and we saw them coming in—slow and easy and all the sudden there's a fireball off his left wing. The sirens went and the rescue trucks scrambled and the rest of us just froze as they managed to get the plane down safe and tried to taxi, but before they could stop fully, there was another explosion and fire swept through—* Oh God, Ben, I could hear them. They were screaming, all of them. We could hear

them. And then they weren't. There was just the roar of the fire and the men outside trying to fight it back. I don't know which was worse to hear—the screams or the godawful crackling of that fire. But I know I'll hear both until the day I die.

I am sorry, love. I shouldn't burden you with this. I don't want you to worry—I'm not in any more danger than I was yesterday. And we check and recheck and check again that everything's all right—Jim really keeps us all in line. And we both know that there is risk and danger and that is important what I'm doing here—

Right? Because at this very moment, I can't think of a single thing that is worth never seeing your smile again.

Tomorrow—tomorrow, I'll be better. Stronger. I'll remember all those things, all those reasons why I'm here doing this.

For tonight, I just wish you were holding me in your arms. You'd hold me and rub my back and help me try to understand what the hell is going on and give me something to bank on, something to trust, something to hold on to while the world around me goes crazy. Because I know it's going to get worse. We're going to lose more men, good men, my friends, and I need to get a grip on how to handle this.

John's wife, Ellie, is giving birth to their first child next month. I want to write her a letter, too.

All my love—all of it, B—forever and always.

P.

Ben didn't know what he was supposed to write in response. He felt certain there were patriotic slogans, about duty and honor and putting the greater good before one's own. But there were songs and movies and poems—all proclaiming the same thing, rallying the troops and heartening the populace.

Instead, Ben wrote simply, "*I am here. For whatever you need, for whatever will help you. I am here.*"

CHAPTER THREE

Weeks stretched into months that went by slowly for Ben, incredibly fast for Pete. Ben wrote Pete every day, Pete wrote when he could. Ben saved every letter—when he was feeling particularly lonely after reading through them, he'd press them to his face and could swear he could smell Pete in them.

> *Dear B—*
>
> *This is it. We graduate tomorrow. Our "pinning ceremony," where we get our wings, is tomorrow night and then we're homebound. I can't believe I'm done. I can't believe I'm coming home. To you. Oh, darling, I can't believe I'll see you soon—am I dreaming?*
>
> *They won't give us any information on when we'll actually arrive in the city—troop trains being what they are, I suspect they don't even know. I have a wild hope that I'll beat this letter back to you, but most likely, it'll be a few more days. I swear, I'll be home as soon as I can.*
>
> *I know you probably would like to meet me at the station, but as I don't know when I'll be there, we'll have to figure something else out. I kind of like the idea of just showing up at home. Don't wait for me—God, please don't sit in the apartment waiting for me. Just leave my key under the mat if you have to go out, and I'll let myself in.*
>
> *I'll see you soon, my love. I cannot wait to hold you and kiss your face and hear you tell me everything you've been up to while I've been gone. I love you.*
>
> *All my love, always.*

P.

P.S. Wouldn't that be something? If you went out to buy milk one morning, and came home and there I was, already asleep on the couch?

* * *

IN FACT, THAT'S ALMOST HOW it happened.

The day Ben received the letter, he refused to leave the apartment, just in case. After three days, Ginger came and dragged him out shopping.

"You need groceries, Williams. Pete's got the appetite of a teenage wildebeest—"

"Wildebeests are over-large antelopes. They don't eat that much, comparatively," he sniffed.

"Oh, quit your arguing." She swatted his arm impatiently. "Fine, a teenaged rhinoceros, then. Regardless, you're going to need food—a lot of food, for when he comes home. Because we all know that once he gets home, you two are not going to be leaving again for quite some time." She nudged him knowingly with her elbow. He glared at her as he slid Pete's key under the welcome mat outside the front door.

They returned a short time later, laden with paper sacks full of groceries, playfully arguing and laughing. Ben's pulse began to race when he realized the deadbolt was no longer locked. A smile burst on his face as he pushed the door open and saw a dusty green duffle bag sitting just to the side of the foyer. Ginger awkwardly grabbed the bags he'd been carrying before he could drop them, as he raced down the hall.

There was Pete, his bare feet propped up on the coffee table, grinning delightedly. Apparently, he'd been home just long enough to shower—he was sitting on the couch with nothing on but a towel around his waist. His dark hair still dripped slightly.

Ben hurled himself at him. Pete caught him and was knocked back against the couch with a muffled "ooof." Ben stretched out on top of him. Neither of them could stop smiling enough to kiss each other properly, or stop kissing enough to smile at each other. Instead, they peppered each other's faces, lips, necks with a million tiny kisses—giggling like schoolboys and then laughing at how much they were giggling.

Ben thought he heard Ginger putting things away in the kitchen. He vaguely knew when she walked into the living room and set something down, entirely unsurprised by their exuberant kissing. He felt her hand on his hair, heard her whisper to Pete, "I'm so happy you're home, honey." Then she slipped away.

Just before their kissing turned serious—just before Pete's towel became superfluous and Ben's clothes were ripped from his body—they parted long enough to realize Ginger had brought in a dinner tray, set with plates of cheese and crackers, a bit of bread, some pickles, two glasses and a bottle of wine. She'd written a card: "Nurse Ginger reminds you that neglecting to eat is not only hazardous to your health, but can have worrying sexual side effects as well."

* * *

THAT EVENING, BETS AND GINGER sat in their living room, listening to the radio and grinned knowingly at each other when a slow rhythmic squeaking began in the ceiling over their heads.

When they heard Pete begin to laugh raucously, infectiously, and Ben join in, Bets turned up the volume on the radio, smilingly affectionately. Their boys.

But her smile faltered. It's so strange what things remind you that time is running out.

* * *

THEY HAD NINE DAYS TOGETHER before Pete had to report to the docks to board the troop carrier that would take him to Europe.

The first two days were spent in bed. Or nearly in bed. Sometimes, they were on the floor. Sometimes, in the bathtub—where they struggled to fit inside at the proper angles and to keep the water from splashing on the floor as they found their rhythm. They broke the chair that usually sat in front of Ben's vanity; apparently, it was not meant to withstand repeated applications of the weight of two grown men.

By the third day, they were nearly satiated with each other. They dressed, finally, and did not immediately undress. Pete was now required to be in uniform at all times—*surely not all times,* Ben had whispered hotly in his ear the first day, and that was when they had to figure out how to sew the regulation buttons back on Pete's shirt. This time, they actually left the apartment for groceries—*man cannot live on love alone,* Pete paraphrased, murmuring into the back of Ben's shoulder as they took the elevator downstairs.

Their groceries bought, their errands run, they returned home. Ben cooked; Pete helped chop and slice and did whatever Ben demanded— which frequently involved *Kiss me, you fool.*

* * *

THE FIFTH DAY, BEN ASKED to see Pete's uniforms they'd picked up from a shop downtown.

"That jacket looks heavy," Ben said, as Pete carefully put everything on in their bedroom. It was late morning and Ben was still curled up under the sheets. Pete's sheepskin bomber jacket and gloves lay on the bed, the wool inside still bright against the dark brown leather outside.

"The plane's not heated, love." Pete deftly buttoned his uniform shirt. "It gets damn cold when we're flying up at altitude—it's so cold, your bare hand instantly freezes to whatever metal you touch. We also have jackets and pants that are actually wired, and they get plugged in and heated electrically."

"But you don't have those now?"

"I get issued those before every flight." Pete tucked his shirt into his light brown uniform pants. "Along with my flak jacket. Which is like armor, almost. It's heavy and it's sheer hell to move around in. We only put it on when we get closer to the target where there'll be—have I explained this yet?"

Ben tried to look calm and nonchalant, despite his hands going cold. The thought of Pete needing armor to keep him safe made his stomach drop. "No. I don't believe you have."

"Well, flak is an anti-aircraft shell. Around places they know will be targets, they shoot these exploding balls up in the sky. If one hits a plane, more's the better, but mainly, it's to be a pain in the ass for the approaching bombers. It explodes and knocks you around. A lot of planes get filled with shrapnel and the crews get hurt. You can't dodge it or you'll be off course and won't be able to drop the bombs on target, so you just have to deal with flying through it," Pete explained, checking over the uniform.

"And do people die from it?" Ben's voice was small.

Pete looked him directly in the eye. "Sometimes. I'm not going to lie to you, B. It's dangerous and deadly. But I'm learning as much as I can, so I can keep myself safe as much as I can—myself, and my crew. "

"So, tell me about this crew of yours." Ben bit his lip as he changed the subject and made a pointed show of stretching himself out lazily in their bed. "Who are these men I have to share you with?"

"First of all, there's not going to be any sharing," Pete said, grimacing in the mirror as he attempted to tie his uniform's recalcitrant necktie. "Borrowing, maybe, but no sharing. Sharing implies a semi-permanent arrangement, and that is not okay with me. I'm all yours."

"Mmm, that's good to know." Ben smiled. "But, what are they *like?* You never really explained them in your letters."

"Well, there's Jim—Jim Livingston; he's my co-pilot. He's steady and calm. It's impossible to rattle him. He doesn't say much, but he keeps track of everything and he always knows what's going on. Nothing surprises him or seems to catch him off-guard. He's a good man."

"And he's from Texas?" Ben asked. "At least, I think that's what you said?"

"Oh yes. A Texas cowboy. He's a lot like John Wayne, except he talks a little faster, when he finally gets around to talking."

His necktie finally knotted to his satisfaction, he slipped on his overseas cap, which looked like a flexible wedge of cloth. He cocked it slightly to one side and ducktailed the back corner. He turned around to show it off.

"Ohhh," breathed Ben. "That is very nice. Very dashing."

Pete grinned. "Thanks, sweetheart."

"Now do the formal one," Ben said eagerly. "And tell me about the rest of the crew."

Pete turned his attention to making sure his pilot's insignia were still pinned properly to his brown wool officer's coat where it hung from the doorframe.

"And then there's Charlie. Charlie Thompson, the bombardier from Maine. He's loud and clumsy and a bit of an oaf, sometimes. But a swell guy with a real good heart." He brushed some lint off his coat. "I was a little worried at first, because he jokes about everything."

"I could see that being a problem."

"But, once we're in the plane, doing our pre-flight checklists, he goes into this mood—almost a trance—and it lasts until the wheels touch the ground again after the flight. He's focused and serious and down to business and precise. I'm glad he's on our crew."

"Sounds likes he's two different people, almost," Ben said.

"I think he just compensates for being so sharp when it's time to work," Pete shrugged. "The rest of the time, he lets himself relax."

"Do you consider him a friend?"

"I probably have the most fun with him. It's impossible not to like him and it's impossible for me not to laugh when he's around." Pete slipped his coat off the hanger and slid it on, buttoning the brass buttons and buckling the cloth belt around his trim waist.

Ben smiled at that. He knew Pete loved to laugh. "And wasn't there a fourth roommate?"

"Bill, yes. Bill Livingston. He's from Chicago, and he's—you have to get used to him. He's opinionated and loud and I thought he was an ass when I first met him." Pete took his service cap, the cardboard stiffener ring removed so the cap will fit comfortably under his headphones when he flies, and placed it on his head, cocking it just slightly.

"He sounds charming," Ben snorted, admiring Pete in the mirror, then sighed. "Oh, I like you in that hat."

"Thanks." Pete grinned, catching Ben's eye in the mirror. He continued. "But, then I got to know him a little bit better. He's opinionated, but he's willing to listen. He just feels really strongly about things, and he has a hard time being mellow. But he's an amazing navigator, sharp and precise and accurate. He's always three steps ahead of the game, always has an answer ready whenever I need it, and he's a swell guy."

"And what about the rest of them?"

"There are six more guys, who're mostly enlisted men. We'll meet up with them when we get to base."

"And, Bill and Jim and Charlie—are they married, do they have families, what's their favorite baseball team, what do they want to be when they grow up?" Ben teased.

"None of us are married, no kids. That's about all I know. Charlie loves the Red Sox, Bill loves the White Sox and Jim and I just hope to get out of every baseball discussion without having to break up a fist-fight between them."

Ben eyed Pete's uniform with a practiced tailor's eye. He sat up straight in bed. "You *do* know that you're wearing at least four different shades of brown, right?"

"Yeah." Pete laughed. "It's all supposed to be 'olive drab,' but since all the officers have to buy them ourselves, none of them are the same. No one's is. It's not a problem."

"Your crew—do they have girls back home?"

"Charlie does, I know. I am not sure about Bill and Jim."

"Do they—do they know about us?" Ben asked quietly.

Pete turned and looked at Ben, serious and sure. "They know I have a sweetheart in New York City, who I love with all my heart and soul."

Ben's smile quivered a bit. Pete never had any trouble telling him what's in his heart.

"Oh, you do now, do you?" Ben teased as he clambered out of their bed, his hair disheveled, in just his pajama bottoms. "You're so sentimental, sometimes."

"Some things are worth being sentimental over. You, for instance."

"Your belt is twisted." Ben stood in front of him, unbuckling Pete's belt and wrapping his arms around Pete's waist to untwist it.

Pete caught Ben's mouth with his own and took the opportunity to kiss him, thoroughly and slowly and completely. Ben, careful and deliberate, took off Pete's clothes, careful not to pop any buttons, careful not to wrinkle, and once Pete was stripped bare, they eased back into bed, delighting in each other, reveling in each other's arms.

* * *

ON THE SIXTH EVENING, THE girls threw a cocktail party in Ginger's honor; she'd just completed her training with the Army Nurse Corps. She and Pete would be taking the same troopship to Europe, though neither knew where they'd be stationed.

After the party, they all went out to the Black Cat. When the band heard it was Pete's last night in town, they urged him to come sing a set with them, and he laughingly complied, crooning away and making the girls swoon. Ben winked at him, and Pete forgot the next line in the song. It was a good night.

When they got home, Ben was surprised to see Pete walk swiftly to the liquor cabinet in their living room and pour himself glasses of whiskey, straight-up—three, four, five—which he slammed back with barely a breath between them. He sat abruptly on the floor, his legs splayed out in front him, his eyes screwed shut.

"It's not helping," he said through gritting teeth.

"What's not helping, baby?" Ben knelt next to him, concerned.

"It's not going away; it's not going away." Pete scrubbed both hands through his hair, dislodging his cap, which fell to the floor next to him.

"What's not going away, sweetheart?" Ben kept his voice quiet and soothing, reaching to loosen Pete's khaki tie.

"I'm afraid, Ben." Pete looked into Ben's eyes, desperately pleading. "I've never been so scared in my entire life, and I don't know how to handle it."

"What are you scared of?" Ben gently asked.

"I'm scared of..." Pete searched Ben's face, finding the courage to let it all tumble out. "I'm was going to say that I'm scared of everything now. But that's not it. I'm not scared of being injured or shot down or captured."

Ben swallowed thickly. He couldn't bear— he couldn't bear the thought.

"I'm not scared of pain. I'm not scared of death, really, even. I'm just scared that I will never be here again, never just sit on this stupid rug with you, never bang my knee on that stupid cabinet door in the kitchen. I'm scared I'm going to miss all the little things that make up our lives. I'm scared that that was the last time I had to remind Ginger's cousin that I don't want to go out with her, that that was the last time I'll order you a whiskey sour at the Cat." He dropped his head, looking miserably into his hands hanging loosely over his knees.

"But I can handle all that—*that* I can deal with. What scares me the worst is the thought of not seeing you again. I can be brave about everything else, Benny. I can. But not seeing you again? That's what's going to kill me. I'm so frightened I will never see you again."

Ben couldn't think of what to say. His mind had a million words, words of comfort, words of reassurance, but his mouth worked soundlessly. He took both of Pete's hands in his, gently holding them.

"You will see me again. I promise, love. I'll be here, I'll be here." He tugged on Pete's hands as he sat down on the floor, pulling Pete into his arms. They sat in silence for a bit.

"You're coming back. Everything's going to be okay, baby. I'll be here, and you'll come back and everything will be wonderful." Ben cooed into Pete's hair, as Pete's sobs rocked them both. "We'll finally take that trip to Miami we've been talking about; we'll do Sunday brunch at Rocky's just like we always do. Everything's going to be okay, baby.

"I'll yell at you about your hair in the tub drain. You'll yell at me about using all the hair pomade." Pete's sobs quieted as Ben continued.

"It'll be just like old times. Nothing's going to change. I'm still going to be yours. You're still going to be mine, right? Right?" Ben nudged Pete's side with his knee. "Hey, Lieutenant Montgomery? Right?"

Pete pulled back, knuckling the last tears out of his eyes. His voice was low and rough, "Right. I'm yours. I always have been and I always will be."

"Good. Now we need to get up, because my ass just fell asleep."

"Oh, I can wake it up." Pete's speech was becoming steadily more slurred.

"You're drunk, Montgomery. *Five* whiskeys in quick succession on a nearly-empty stomach? You're not going to be able—"

"Can, too."

"Cannot."

"Can, too!"

"Peter, seriously, my legs are tingling, we need to get up."

"I can make your legs tingle."

"Yes, darling. Always. Just not now. Come on." Ben levered the two of them upright.

"Ben?"

"Yes?"

"Thank you. And I love you. And thank you—"

"Let's get you to bed, flyboy." They began to shuffle towards the bedroom, Pete's arm wrapped tightly over Ben's supporting shoulder.

"Benny? I think I'm drunk."

"You are certainly drunk, Mr. Montgomery."

"Yes, I am certainly drunk Mr. Montgomery. That's me."

* * *

THE MORNING OF THE SEVENTH day, Pete took an aspirin and a Bloody Mary for his hangover, then ventured into the city on his own. He returned late that afternoon with a large leather folio, which he promptly handed to Ben, pulling him out of the kitchen where he'd been baking.

"What's this?" Ben wiped the flour off his hands before taking it.

"This has all been in the works for a while now, but I went to visit George Abernathy, the family attorney, to pick it all up. Just open it."

They sat on the couch next to each other, Ben on the edge. He pulled out the documents slowly one by one.

"Well, first, that's my will." Pete sighed as Ben flinched and hastily put it down on the coffee table in front of them.

"You don't need to read it now. But you should know that I named you the executor of my estate."

"Shouldn't that be a relative? Your brother? Family?" Ben stammered.

"You *are* my family, Benjamin." Pete put his hand over Ben's and looked at him intently.

Ben smiled faintly at him.

"I don't have to read it right now, do I?"

"No. You don't. Not now. Just don't lose it."

"I won't." Ben smiled wider at the teasing. He rarely lost anything—it was Pete who was constantly searching for things he'd had only moments before.

The next document was nearly an inch thick, the pages all clipped together.

"What's this?"

"This is my stock portfolio. Well, copies of the paperwork for it, anyway. I've had my broker add you as the sole beneficiary. If anything happens to me, all the stocks and bonds I own go to you."

"This… this seems like there's a lot…" Ben waved his hands at the paperwork.

"It is. My grandmother's been giving me stock every year since I was born. This is just the stock I currently control. When I turn thirty, I gain control of the rest of my trust. If anything happens to me before that time, it is still held in trust, until you turn thirty."

Ben's hands were trembling as he pulled out the next documents.

"The apartment is still in my Uncle Ernest's name. They didn't change the deed when I inherited it, because I wasn't of age then, but George is working on it now. He'll send it to you—it'll have your name on it, as well. And the deed to the beach house. Your name is on it now, too."

"Peter—" Ben shook his head, unable to speak further.

"I just need to know that you're taken care of, Ben. I need to know you're going to be okay, no matter what."

"I *will* be okay, no matter what."

Pete sighed. "I know, baby, I know. I just need to know that you've got a roof over your head and money in the bank. I need to know you're taken care of. I won't be able to go without knowing that. I can't do anything about my personal bank account, except to stipulate that whatever money is in there be forwarded to our joint account, in the event of my death."

He sighed. "I also can't do anything about the Army."

"What about the Army?" Ben's brow furrowed.

"I can't designate you as my next-of-kin. If I'm injured, or worse, they're not going to notify you."

Ben swallowed hard.

"They notify my parents. And it took some real talking and some yelling, but for what I think is the first time in my life, I had an actual long, hard conversation with them, on the telephone from George's office. My dad threw up his hands in disgust and left to go golfing at the club like he always does, but I think my mother understands now that I'm not coming back to Pennsylvania to marry Dinah Martin or any of her bridge club's daughters. I think my going off to—to war, has made her think about what's truly important. And she's realized that *I'm important*, and you are important to me. So she's sworn, on the life of her mother and her favorite sapphire earrings, that she will contact you as soon as she hears anything." Pete leaned against the pillows of the couch, stretching one arm behind Ben, pulling him close.

"*If* she hears anything," Ben corrected, firmly. "*If*, baby."

"Right. *If.*" Pete smiled gently.

The folio was empty.

"Is that it?" Ben asked. "All the serious stuff?"

"That's it. Are you okay with it all?"

"It's overwhelming and I have this feeling that I should probably object and say it's too much to accept and refuse it all."

"But, you're not going to, right?" Pete looked anxious.

"I'm not going to. I know if I do, you're just going to keep arguing and arguing. And I know you and your reasons. So I'm just going to say thank you. And I love you so much."

"I love you, too, baby."

* * *

THE EIGHTH DAY WAS SPENT repacking Pete's bag. Though he'd only been home for a few days, somehow his things were strewn all over the apartment. Ben joked that Pete's clothes always exploded off him and his things were worse. Ben showed Pete how to best fold his uniform to minimize wrinkling and keep the creases sharp. Pete showed Ben how he was now required to roll his socks—an exercise in discipline from flight training.

On the ninth day, Bets and Ben took Pete and Ginger to the docks. Massive ships painted a somber gray bobbed at anchor, waiting to take on troops and ferry them across the Atlantic. A mass of people milled about, soldiers finding which ship to report to, friends and loved ones not wanting to lose sight of them too soon. The mood of the crowd was somber but proud. There were no hysterical goodbyes. No outward tears. Several exuberant signs of affection—soldiers knocking the hats off their girls as they swept them into their arms and kissed them. Pete stood close to Ben, reaching out with his pinky to hook it around Ben's. They didn't speak. Bets and Ginger determinedly chatted animatedly—pointing out attractive soldiers and sailors and giggling.

The final bell sounded for all military personnel to board the hulking ship. Ginger hugged Ben tightly and kissed him loudly on the cheek. She took off one glove and rubbed the trace of her lipstick away, smiling fondly.

"Chin up, mate. I'll keep my eye on him as long as I can," she said softly, lightly bopping him on the nose with her gloved finger.

As Ginger hugged Bets, Pete spun his hand to grip Ben's fiercely, just for a moment. Then he let go and he stepped away. He turned, and anyone watching from afar would think they were only casual acquaintances. Anyone who could see his tortured eyes would know otherwise.

"Well, so long, Ben," Pete said, tried to keep his voice light. "I'll be seeing you."

"Yes," Ben managed. "I'll be seeing you."

With a quick, fierce hug for Bets, Pete spun smartly on his heel and walked quickly to the gangplank, Ginger striding swiftly beside him.

Long minutes passed before Bets and Ben finally spotted them amongst the soldiers leaning over a guardrail on one of the upper decks. They were together, waving like fools so they could be spotted. Ben and Bets waved back frantically. The giant ship blared its horn and pulled ever so slowly away from the dock. Pete continued waving like a fool, pausing only to gently press his fingers to his lips once before smiling sadly and waving again.

Ben, back on shore, mirrored him exactly.

Tears streaming down her face, Bets wrapped her arms around Ben's waist and clung to him fiercely.

Anyone watching them would think it was Ben holding Bets up, and not the other way around.

CHAPTER FOUR

THE FIRST DAY OUT, IT was raining and cold, and Pete was fine with that. He felt gray and gloomy, himself. Ginger fussed over him, much to the amusement of his cabinmates. Under Pete's bleak eye, they proceeded to flirt with her outrageously—and she flirted back. After dinner, they all gathered in their cramped cabin and carefully drew the blackout curtains. They boosted her up to the top of one of the bunk beds, and she kicked her shoes off and swung her feet and told dirty jokes that had them all in stitches until it was curfew and she had to scurry back to the nurse's quarters.

Pete didn't sleep well that night. The drone and vibration of the ship's huge engines made him nauseous and hurt his ears. He missed Ben. He wanted Ben curled around him, wanted to press his cold feet on Ben's shins, to feel Ben's breath tickling his ear. *Ben, Ben, Benny, oh God, I want Ben.*

He woke the next day, sandy-eyed and grumpy. He hated sleeping on the top bunk. It was still fucking cold. It was still fucking raining. It was still fucking loud everywhere. His feet were starting to feel numb with the constant reverberation of the decks.

He was overly curt with Charlie when it was time to head to the mess hall for lunch and he felt bad. He tried to be pleasant at dinner. He tried. He thought he didn't really succeed, but everyone seemed to appreciate the effort.

The next day was emergency drills. U-Boats, deadly and dangerous German submarines, hunted the Atlantic for merchant convoys, bent on choking off their enemies' supplies, in the hopes of bringing England to its knees. Sinking troop convoys was not their primary purpose, but it did happen. Pete and his shipmates drilled emergency protocols over and over again. Privately, he thought that getting into a lifeboat when your ship had been torpedoed and sunk from underneath you was similar to continuing to swim after the shark has bitten your leg off—but he wasn't going to say anything. He drilled, conscientiously, diligently and with care.

The next day was sunny and bright. Nagging and yanking on his ankles, Ginger forcibly removed him from his high bunk and pulled him up to the top deck. He was still moody; he was still feeling dark blue and full of storm clouds, but he let himself be dragged along. Ginger marched them to the prow—the wind whipping her hair wildly, making their eyes tear and their noses run.

Ginger hunched in her jacket and shoved her hands deep in the pockets. She sniffed from time to time, but didn't say a word. Silent as well, Pete leaned his crossed arms atop the gunwales, looking steadily out toward the horizon. Out of the corner of his eye, he studied her. Her freckles were lost in the pink the wind was whipping into her skin. She was his "Red"—always game for anything he suggested, always jumping in with both feet, loving him, loving Ben, loving Bets so fiercely. He felt a rush of affection for her. He swallowed hard and turned his head to take in the rest of the ships and the planes flying overhead.

"How many boats does it take to make an armada?"

Ginger huffed a laugh. "More than this, I imagine."

"What about a flotilla? Are we a flotilla?"

"Petey, you're not a pirate."

"… That's what you think," Pete muttered.

Ginger laughed and nudged him roughly with her shoulder. He stumbled, laughed and recovered, then nudged her back.

"Everything's going to be okay, Pete."

* * *

BEN'S TAILOR SHOP WAS ON a quiet street just a block from the apartment he shared with Pete. He'd apprenticed with a larger, more famous tailor on a busy street in a fashionable part of town. His hard work, impeccable style and precise stitching had earned the love and loyalty of several society patrons—Mrs. Horowitz, Mrs. Crumpelbak and a Vanderbilt cousin—along with their circles of friends. When he had decided to open his own shop, they had followed him gladly.

His work ethic, his commitment to quality, his fresh ideas—they made him a name. A quiet name—not splashed across billboards or spoken on the radio, but he was *known*. When a son needed his first suit to make a good impression, when mother gave a debutante that impeccable dress that didn't quite flatter her, when the occasion called for something with a certain understated *je ne sais quoi*—see Ben.

Ben loved designing, he really did. He loved to hold a bolt of fabric and try to figure out what it wanted to be. He loved sketching designs. He loved finally seeing the finished product—loved to see it on someone the first time they tried it on and it fit and *oh God Ben! I love it! Look! I never thought I'd say this, but I'm pretty, aren't I? Oh, thank you, Ben!*

He also loved alterations—changing a garment so it actually fit and flattered the person wearing it. Raising Mrs. Gardner's hemline just a fraction of an inch—showing off her gorgeous legs, and making her feel ten years younger. Fixing the bodice on Mrs. Polley's blouse—finally flattering her figure and bringing a smile back to her face. Hemming the pants of Mr. Christopher's new tuxedo for his gallery opening—he'd lost weight and his old one didn't fit any more.

You could tell a lot about a person while measuring someone's inseam. It was intimate, to say the least. Ben was always politely distant, always professional, always quick. Most men would blush uncomfortably, stare at the opposite wall and try to pretend the procedure didn't bother them.

Some men, though, would watch Ben intently as he knelt in front of them. Ben would take his measuring tape from around his neck, pretending not to notice the blatant tightening of the pants in front of him. He'd measure carefully, so as not to have to repeat it—and that would be it. He didn't fool around with his customers, no matter how attractive they were, no matter how their thighs flexed under their trousers, no matter how impressive he found things while measuring their inseams. He didn't fuck his customers.

Well, there had been Phillip, that's true—but he didn't really count as a customer, as they'd been casual friends for a while. Phillip, smiling shyly, had walked into Ben's shop with a pair of pants that he insisted needed shortening. Ben had taken one look at the hem and realized it was a ruse. Yes, he had taken the initiative to take very thorough and repeated measurements: cupping and rolling and stroking and, okay, yes, that time, there was fucking involved.

And then there had been George. That time, he counted as a mistake. He'd never met George before he walked through Ben's shop door, a garment bag of brand new suits for his new job slung casually over his shoulder. George had been gorgeous. Ben had been nervous. George had been curious. Ben had gotten over his nerves quickly. He'd still been buttoning his pants when George walked out the door. When he came to pick up his completed suits, Ben had spied the wedding ring that had been missing from his hand earlier, and didn't answer George's calls again.

Of course, that had all been before Pete. Pete, who'd driven all thoughts and desires of any other man completely out of Ben's head. Who was everything to Ben, absolutely everything.

Pete, who had asked one day, "But, Ben? Who hems *your* pants?"

Ben had proceeded to give him a rigorous training in tailoring and measuring properly. That had been the day they had discovered that the tailor's stool Ben had for hemming meant that Pete didn't have to crouch quite so low when kneeling to suck Ben's cock.

Ben leaned back in his chair, stretching his arms over his head. He couldn't afford to be distracted while altering this evening gown—there might be a war, but society still went on.

He'd closed the shop hours ago, locked the door and drawn the blinds. He often worked late to finish up important pieces and sometimes fell asleep at the shop to stumble home in the early morning light.

Tonight, there was Mrs. Sandberg's dress to do. He could get a start on those trousers. He could play around with that jacket he'd been designing. Anything to keep from going home to the empty apartment.

He pushed himself back from the sewing machine, stood and stretched some more. He put the coffee pot on the small stove—he definitely needed some coffee to get through this.

The thought of Pete, the memory of Pete's mouth on him here in this room, Pete's body covering his own, had got him hard. This wasn't going to work. He wasn't going to be able to concentrate. He snapped off the gas, put the coffee pot back on the shelf, donned his coat and hat, stepped out into the wind and locked the door carefully behind him. He walked to their building and nodded at Thomas who stood in front of the doors.

He unlocked their door, flicked the hallway light switch on and strode immediately to the radio, turning it on as well. He always had the radio on while he was home alone. Silence these days drove Ben mad. Their apartment was stiflingly quiet now; Ben could hear his own pulse in his ears and he hated it. He didn't care what was on the radio, news, music, dramas—he didn't care. Just enough background noise so he could pretend he wasn't there alone.

He turned off the lights he'd just turned on. He went to their bed— the bed that was slowly losing the scent of Pete—and touched himself, desperately stroking, pretending it was Pete's hands he felt, not his own. He came, gasping and writhing, his face pressed into Pete's pillow.

He left the radio on all night.

* * *

Dear B—

We're here, safe and sound!

Not much time to write at the moment—but I wanted to let you know as soon as my feet touched dry land. Everything's fine here. I'm about to catch the transport to my base (I can't tell you where) where I get to meet the rest of my crew and our plane. Secretly, I think she's mine.

Ginger's assigned to the main hospital nearby—she's made me promise I won't see her there in any official capacity, though I'm welcome to come and have tea with her on her days off.

Did you know she's a card shark? I sure as hell didn't—how the hell did I not know that? I never would have agreed to play poker with her if I did. She beat everyone on the boat. She's got enough money now to live like an empress.

Incidentally, do you think you could mail her three pairs of stockings and a lipstick in a flattering shade? I ran out of money and had to give her an I.O.U.

I love you I love you I love you I love you.

And I miss you a hell of a lot.

All my love, always.

P.

P.S. Do you think you could go to the library and find out how many ships make up an armada vs a flotilla? It's a matter of great consternation and debate around here.

* * *

My darling P—

You can't know how happy I am to hear from you. I've been having nightmares of enemy submarines and icebergs and imagining a whole host of things that could have gone wrong in your crossing. It's good to know you're safe.

I made good on your I.O.U to Ginger and mailed her the stockings and lipstick and a few other things. You should be getting a similar package (sans stockings and lipstick) as well. I hope the cake makes it there—Evelyn swears it's the same recipe her mother used to send her father when he was overseas.

I'm keeping busy. I've been giving Bets cooking lessons—which has gone just about as well as you imagine. I've taken on some Red Cross sewing.

I can't think of anything else to write except how I miss you and think of you all the time and I'm really trying not to be miserable and yesterday I actually laughed for the first time since you've been gone. I miss you and I love you.

All my love, darling, every last bit of it.

Me.

P.S. I asked Mrs. Patterson at the library. There is no set number for either a flotilla or an armada. Both words are used interchangeably by civilians, though it seems generally considered that they are both smaller than a "fleet."

* * *

"OH, THAT IS NOT HOW you're going to want to file that paperwork," a voice came over Pete's shoulder as he stood in the camp clerk's office, squinting as bright light poured in the windows.

"Pardon me?" Pete asked, turning to find a short man with salt and pepper curls smiling up at him.

"Don't submit them all together in a clump like that. He'll have a stroke. If I may?" He held his hands out for the stack of paperwork in Pete's hand.

Pete smiled and shrugged, handing off the sheaf.

"Form 1's, they go in this basket, and Form 1-A's, they go in this basket over here. Do not mix them up," the stranger said sternly. "Just don't do it."

"Okay." This was Pete's first time turning in the papers he was responsible for filing—the flight data form, ensuring that everyone onboard the Redhead was properly credited with flight hours, and the flight report, detailing how the B-17 bomber was operating. It all seemed different from flight school.

"Form 5—that's your crew's individual flight records—just be sure they're all signed before they get here. If they're not, submit them when he's not in the building; otherwise, it's your ass on the line for it."

"When *who's* not in the building?" Pete was bewildered. Any number of airmen were scrambling through the office on their way to different places, and none of them looked particularly threatening.

"Corporal Johnson," the man said, briefly closing his eyes, slightly shaking his head. "He's a… he's a very fine soldier. He's very particular about the way things are done, and when things are *not* done properly, he can be excitable."

The man slipped the last of the paperwork in the proper basket and took Pete's elbow, steering him swiftly out of the office and into the brilliant gray cloud-covered light that signified morning in England. "Actually, he's a pimply-faced, insufferable, self-important wet blanket."

Pete choked back a laugh. "Tell me how you really feel about him."

The man groaned, then laughed. "We don't have the time. But, to be fair, things are running smoothly around here for once since he's been assigned to HQ, so I, for one, am willing to put up with a few tantrums here and there. Plus, I've figured out how he wants it done and I make sure to do it that way every single time, and so Corporal Johnson and I have not had an altercation in weeks. I advise you to do the same, sir."

The man walked them briskly toward the mess hall, opening the door swiftly and bowing at Pete to go ahead of him, both of them sweeping off their crush caps off as they entered and stood in line for lunch.

"I'm Glenn, by the way," the stranger said, grinning. "Glenn Forsythe."

"Pete Montgomery." Pete held out his hand and grinned back as Glenn shook it firmly.

"My girl's the Queen of Tarts out there." Glenn jerked his thumb towards the airfield.

"Mine's the Riveting Redhead," Pete started. "We just got here."

"Oh, I know. New plane, new crew, everyone's been talking. Word has it that you're a crooner…"

"I sing some, yes. Nothing big or important, just in little clubs here and there."

"Excellent. There's a dance coming up, and sometimes the singers they bring in are just—" Glenn shuddered.

Further conversation was dampened by their travel through the chow line, as the cooks behind the counter filled their trays. They poured themselves coffee and found a table, then dug into their food. It wasn't home cooking, but it was good and hot, and they ate in companionable silence.

"So, you're a singer, you're new here. What else?" Glenn wiped his lips fastidiously with a napkin.

Pete looked down at his tray, smiling brightly. "Ummm, I'm from Philadelphia."

"Philly," Glenn interrupted. "Let me guess: your family owns a coal mine..."

"Well, actually, yes." Pete laughed. "How did you know that?"

"I just know. It's a gift."

"And you? Where are you from?"

"Chicago—"

"And your family owns a diamond mine?" Pete teased.

"No, my family's in aluminum, actually. Bit of a boom there, at the moment, actually." Glenn scraped his chair back to lounge negligently with one arm folded over the back of it, his green eyes twinkling. "You have a wife and kids back there in Philadelphia?"

"No wife, no kids. And I actually live in New York."

"Oooh, leaving the nest behind to spread your wings and fly. I bet Mumsy-dear is trying to lure you back to the flock with society debutantes and marriageable virgins galore."

Pete laughed. "Mmm, she used to. But I'm happy in New York."

It was easy talking to Glenn, a sparkling back and forth banter that was effortless right from the beginning. Pete appreciated his dry wit, his pointed barbs. He felt at ease with him—certainly more at ease with Glenn than with anyone else on the base, other than his crew. He appreciated the insights into life on base: how to handle certain personalities in charge; which nurses to avoid entanglements with; how to stay in the good graces of their superior officers, the company clerk, the head cook and the sergeant in charge of the motor pool.

They stayed in the mess hall most of the afternoon talking, before taking a walk around in the afternoon sun, enjoying a cigarette along the way. Glenn introduced him to everyone they met, and Pete carefully made note of people's faces—he hated to have to be reminded of people's names.

"We're actually shacked up together, you know," Glenn informed him as they walked into their barracks. "I was out when you all arrived, but I do believe you'll find I'm four bunks down on the left."

"I do hope you don't snore," Pete teased as they took off their coats and hung them up before loosening their ties.

"Oh, Captain Montgomery, you know as well as I do, a true gentleman never snores." Glenn threw himself dramatically on his bunk, face up and beatifically closing his eyes. "Now, hush. I'm an old man and I need my respite after our afternoon constitutional."

Pete huffed a laugh, lying down on his own bunk—the springs protesting under his weight, the supports thumping into the wall lightly as he shifted. The mattress was lumpy and thin; the springs squeaked with just his breathing. *Good thing I'm not sharing it with Ben*, he thought wryly, and a pang struck his chest.

He thought about Ben wrinkling up his nose and laughing at him, and fell asleep to Glenn's delicate snoring.

* * *

WEEKS TURNED INTO MONTHS. BEN and Pete exchanged happy adoring letters. Ben sent Pete reminders of home. Pete sent Ben things he picked up in little shops, antique stores—a silver locket pin, a shell-thin teacup painted with violets, a heart-shaped rock he found near the flight line one day after a mission. Ben told Pete the mundane details of his life—the funny stories he would have told him over the dinner table. Pete told Ben as much as he could about his missions, his love of flying, his devotion to his wonderful crew and theirs to him.

Ben slowly re-learned how to be alone: how to remember to not make a double pot of coffee; how to buy only enough bread for one, instead of two; how to fall asleep without someone to hold onto. It was difficult, and he struggled every day, every lonely night alone in their bed, at their dinner table, in all the places they'd been together, trying to keep moving, to keep from sinking into despair. It was a struggle every day, but he did it.

He often found himself awash with memories. Banging his hip into the corner of the sideboard that stuck out just a bit too far reminded him of the day they'd found it at a shop, fallen in love with it and wrestled it home and into place without realizing it was too deep for the space, and how they'd had no choice but to sit on the floor and laugh. He could see them sitting there, as plain as day.

Getting ready for bed one night and realizing the pajama bottoms he'd put on were too tight around his hips, too short in the leg. They were Pete's, which made him laugh and ache at the same time. They rarely wore pajamas, but he remembered the first time Pete had worn *his* pajamas.

It had been the first time since they'd met that they'd been apart for more than a day. It had been two days since they'd last spent the night together. They'd gone out to see a show, then wrapped themselves up in each other in the bed at Pete's apartment. The next morning, Pete had insisted Ben take his umbrella for his walk to the tailor shop while he himself dashed off into the rain, with his briefcase held futilely over his head, to catch his bus to work.

With a gala at the Met approaching later that month, Ben had found he was swamped with fittings and alterations, and Mrs. Vanderhooeven suddenly insisted on a gown with an entirely new design. He'd phoned Pete at work that afternoon, anxious about breaking their plans. But there had been no way he could get everything done if he didn't work late that night, and perhaps the night after. Pete had assured him he understood; he was also up to his ears in work.

They'd only known each other for six weeks, but Ben had felt somehow off without Pete to wake up to, without Pete to come home to. Without Pete in his bed, he had slept uneasily. It had been as if something essential was missing, something Ben hadn't known he was missing until it wasn't there.

HE'D FINALLY CAUGHT UP AT work and was waiting eagerly for their night out. The elevator bell had chimed in the narrow hallway outside his apartment and he'd flown to open the door. There Pete had stood, in the midst of wiping his nose with his handkerchief, his hair windblown, looking slightly rumpled and disheveled and handsome.

"Hi." Ben felt as though he could finally take a deep breath.

Pete smiled back. "Hi, yourself."

"Please come in." Ben opened the door wider, gesturing with one arm.

"I'm sorry." Pete smiled ruefully as he ducked inside. "I felt like I should bring you some flowers or something. I'm not really sure what to do, on a proper date, or—"

"A proper date?" Ben raised an eyebrow and laughed gently. "Is this a proper date, now?"

"Yes," Pete said earnestly. "A proper date, and I'm picking you up for it, and we're all gussied up for it, and I'm just going to warn you that I'm going to be fresh and try for a goodnight kiss when I drop you off later."

"Then I will just warn you that I will let you have a goodnight kiss later, but only if you promise that our proper date will lead to some improper activities after said kissing." Ben looked archly over his shoulder, taking his coat off the coat rack near the door.

"Oh, really now?" Pete's face flushed as he took Ben's coat to help him into it, and straightened his scarf. He wrapped his arms around Ben's waist, tugging him closer. "I have missed you, Mr. Williams."

"And I have missed you, Mr. Montgomery," Ben said as he straightened Pete's tie.

"It's been a horrible day at work, and I have been counting the hours until we could go to this movie tonight." Pete leaned in for a kiss.

"It's not just a movie, you fool." Ben teasingly ducked out of the way to correct him, keeping his arms firmly around Pete. "It's a premiere. All the stars will be there. *Lana Turner* will be there. Everyone will be there."

"Including us," Pete finished, pecking a quick kiss on Ben's lips. "But we need to leave now if we want to have any hope of getting through the crowds."

"Are you feeling all right?" Ben frowned.

"Absolutely," Pete said, staunchly, clearing his throat. "Let's get this show on the road."

"Are you sure? You feel warm."

"I'm always warm when you're around," Pete teased. "You make me hot."

"Peter." Ben put the back of his hand to Pete's forehead. "I think you have a fever."

"I always have a fever for you."

Ben giggled. "Stop it, you idiot. You're sick."

"I am not." He sneezed violently, three times in succession, whipping out his handkerchief just in time.

"You are, too. I'm going to get the thermometer."

"Oh, please, don't," Pete said, plaintively. "Who knows when one of your clients will give you tickets to a movie premiere again—a movie premiere that Lana Turner, herself, will be at—and we don't need to miss it because I've got a little tickle in my throat."

"I'm going to take your temperature, and if you have a fever, we are staying here. I wouldn't enjoy being there, knowing you're miserable."

"I'm not miserable, I just have a headache."

"A headache? And what else?" Ben started unbuttoning his coat.

"And a sore throat. But, a little one."

"And you've been sneezing." Ben walked briskly down his little hallway towards bathroom and began rummaging in his medicine chest. "And I bet there's been coughing, as well."

"Not much coughing." Pete sat heavily on the nearby back of the couch, determined not to take off his coat and admit defeat until after his temperature had been taken. Ben returned, briskly flicking the thermometer.

"Open," he directed.

"I don't want—"

"Open, or there's no kissing for a whole week."

Pete hurriedly opened his mouth obediently, earning a chuckle from Ben.

"No talking, now." Ben began untying Pete's scarf, unbuttoning his coat and taking his hat out of his hands. Pete looked disgruntled and unhappy.

"It's all right, darling," Ben soothed. "We'll stay here and I'll make you some soup, and listen to the radio, and I'll take care of you."

Pete frowned, keeping the thermometer's glass tube firmly tucked in his lips, and shook his head.

"I know, darling, I know. But, honestly, you look just awful. Your color's dreadful."

Pete growled behind the thermometer.

"You look miserable, Pete. Not like the gorgeous, happy and healthy man you usually are." Ben coaxed him out of his coat and loosened his tie for him. "Please, let's stay here and let me take care of you."

Pete frowned again, not ready to give up, shaking his head and wincing as the action aggravated his headache.

Ben watched the time, finally taking the thermometer out of Pete's mouth and holding it up to the light to read it.

"A hundred and two, Pete." Ben clicked his tongue. "That is a fever, my dear."

"But I don't want you to miss this. Why don't you go by yourself and I'll head home—"

"Don't you dare even mention it. We are staying here, together, and you are going to let me take your shoes off, and hang your coat up and then you are going to lie there on the couch while I go heat up some soup for the both of us."

"You're a little bit of a scary nurse. I'm scared to misbehave." Pete toed off his shoes, letting his coat sleeves drop off his arms.

"I am a scary nurse. A scary nurse who will not hesitate to spank your bottom if you misbehave, so don't you cross me, Peter Montgomery." Ben narrowed his eyes, trying to look stern as he took Pete's suit jacket off and draped it over a nearby chair.

"Getting my ass spanked by a gorgeous man is not necessarily a behavioral deterrent." Pete grinned unrepentantly as Ben slid his tie off.

"Just get your ass on the couch, Montgomery. We can discuss recreational spankings once you're feeling better."

Pete flopped gracelessly on the couch. "Really?"

"If you like." Ben grinned, before hurrying into the kitchen. He emptied a can of soup into a saucepan, lit the stove and set the pan on to heat. He toasted a few slices of bread and poured orange juice into two glasses: not a gourmet meal, but it might tempt Pete into eating.

Pete's face was pale and clammy, and his hand shook slightly as he slowly raised a spoonful of soup to his mouth.

"Can I help?" Ben asked softly from where he sat next to Pete on the couch.

Pete shook his head woefully. "No, I think I can manage, thank you."

"Here, love. Try it like this," Ben offered, gently. He handed Pete the bowl of soup, keeping hold of it until he was sure Pete had a good grip on it. He pushed the tray out of the way and stacked several pillows on Pete's lap, high enough so the soup bowl wasn't far from his lips, and tucked a napkin in under his chin.

"I'm so sorry, Ben," Pete whispered, as Ben shook two aspirins out of the bottle. "That you have to do this."

"Hey, now." Ben smoothed the hair out of Pete's eyes. "There's no need to apologize."

"But you're missing seeing Lana Turner, in person."

"Oh, who cares? It's not like I'll be able to go over and have a conversation with her. And I'm getting to take care of you."

"What an honor," Pete snorted, taking the pills with sips of juice.

"It is an honor. I bet you don't let anyone see you like this. When you're sick, I bet you hide in your apartment all by yourself until you're feeling better. I bet you don't call anyone to come help you."

"There isn't really anyone who would want to see me like this." Pete stared down at his soup. "I've never really had anyone I could call."

"Well, now you've got me. You can call me, anytime, and I'll come help you."

Pete smiled at him, a small, quiet smile, though it spread to his eyes, which blinked drowsy and dreamy.

"You're looking tired, love. Let me go get you some pajamas to change into, before you fall asleep in your soup."

Ben hurried into his bedroom, pulled two pairs of his pajamas from his bureau and quickly changed into one of them.

From his doorway, he could just see Pete, whose head drooped, carefully spooning broth into his mouth. There was a sharp crease between his eyebrows; his face was tensely set against what must be a raging headache. He had been putting on a good show, but clearly, he was quite ill.

As Ben walked back to the couch with an extra blanket, he turned off the lamp and saw Pete's face relax just a fraction in the dimmer light.

"Here you go, love." Ben handed him the pajamas and set the soup bowl aside. "Would you like some help getting into them?"

"No," Pete said softly. "I think I can manage by myself."

He stood up and stumbled on his way toward the bathroom.

"You could just change here," Ben offered. "Unless you're feeling newly shy, or something."

Pete glanced down at himself and huffed a laugh. In the end, it had been helpful having Ben nearby to help steady him as he changed into the pajamas. Pete's broader shoulders made the buttons stretch tight across his chest, but his lankier hips and shorter legs meant the pants were loose on him. He chuckled weakly as he rolled the waistband to keep the hems from puddling around his ankles.

"If you're trying to imply something about my ass…" Ben began, teasingly.

"The only thing I would like to imply about your ass is that it is perfection incarnate." Pete sat down heavily, tipping his head to rest on the back of the couch. "And I would like to have my hands on it at the first possible opportunity."

Ben laughed and rolled his eyes affectionately. "You're ill, darling. I promise, as soon as you're better, you can put your hands wherever you like. Now lie down, for goodness sake."

He helped Pete swing his feet up on the couch, arranged the pillows more comfortably and tucked the blanket in around him. He snapped on the radio set, turning the dial until he found a show just beginning.

"*The Adventures of Superman* should be on soon." Pete's voice was hoarse. "Have you heard it yet?"

"No, I haven't." Ben tried to perch on the edge of the couch.

"It hasn't been on very long. But it's good." Pete sat up a bit, letting Ben slide in before leaning back across him. It had taken them a bit of maneuvering to find the most comfortable position, but by the time the program started, Ben was stretched out, precariously balanced on the edge, Pete's head on his chest. He felt the heat of Pete's fever through his shirt, and reached up to brush the hair off his forehead.

One radio show had shifted into another, then another. Pete shivered when his fever broke, and Ben pulled the blankets up. He coaxed Pete to drink some more juice, then helped him settle back afterwards, but Pete shifted restlessly.

"Hey," Ben whispered. "Would you like to move to the bed?"

Pete nodded, looking exhausted and frail. Ben fervently hoped this was just a cold and not influenza.

"Come on, then." Ben stood, reaching out both hands to help Pete stand up and holding him steady when he'd wobbled with dizziness. "Let's get you to bed."

He led Pete to the left side of the bed, where Pete had slept the last time he'd fallen asleep here. He couldn't remember if Pete had shown a preference for either side. The few times they'd been here together, there hadn't been a lot of sleeping going on.

He pulled up the blankets and tucked them snugly under Pete's chin and slid into bed next to him.

"Would you—" Pete's voice was almost gone. "Would you mind just holding me?"

Ben slid closer as Pete turned on his side, fitting his body against Pete's, stretching out and slipping his arm across Pete's waist. Pete snuggled back against him.

It was overly warm, and Pete's hair tickled his nose. Ben felt odd, as if something wasn't quite right, then laughed. Whenever they'd spent the night with each other, they'd never worn pajamas. The overly warm, odd feeling came because he had been used to feeling Pete's naked skin against his.

"What's so funny?" Pete mumbled.

"This. You and me. Like this," Ben said quietly. "You're in my bed, you're wearing my pajamas that don't fit you, your nose is running like a faucet and you look like hell. But I'm just happy you're here."

"Yeah?" Pete's voice was muffled by the pillow.

"I… I like this. I mean, I wish you weren't sick, I wish you felt better, but I'm happy you're letting me see you when you're sick and you look like hell. It means a lot to me that you're here, you're letting me in."

"I look like hell, eh?" Pete rolled over slightly, just enough to see him with one eye. "You keep repeating that, and I don't know if I should be offended or not."

"You do look like hell." Ben grinned. "Your face is clammy, your nose is red and your hair is, frankly, just a mess."

"Gee, thanks." Pete rolled back, and Ben tightened his arm around him as Pete snuggled back against him.'

They lay in silence for a bit, Pete's breath faintly whistling and wheezing.

"Hey, Pete?" Ben whispered.

"Yeah."

"What would you say if I said I loved you right now?"

Pete rolled in his arms again, looking back over his shoulder, staring at him, eyes narrowed. Just a few moments before, Ben had felt a rush of adrenaline, a thrill that had gone through him when he'd realized he was in love with Pete. He'd felt a rush of fear, a sudden misgiving: What if Pete didn't feel the same way? What if Pete was horrified? What if he jumped up out of bed and ran out the door? Ben couldn't help how he felt. He was in love with Pete, he had no doubt about it. But maybe telling him so soon was too much. It was too much, too early, and Ben bit his lip anxiously, bracing himself for the rejection that was sure to follow.

"Is that something you're likely to say?" Pete's voice was hoarse as he turned over fully, looking straight into Ben's eyes.

"Yes. I—" Ben gulped. "I love you, Pete."

Pete's eyes fluttered gently closed, as he swallowed hard. "I love you, too, Ben. So much."

Ben wrinkled his nose against a prickling in his eyes and bit his lip hard. "I love you, Ben," Pete whispered, again. "God, that feels so good to say."

Ben chuckled. "It does, doesn't it?"

Pete erupted in an unceremonious sneezing fit, sending Ben into a gale of laughter. He grabbed a hanky from his nightstand and handed it to him with a flourish, barely letting Pete wipe his nose before kissing him soundly.

"No kissing," Pete warned between kisses. "You're going to get sick."

"I don't care. I need to kiss you," Ben said. "And besides, if I get sick, you'll take care of me, right?"

"No." Pete kissed his chin, his cheeks, his eyelids. "I won't."

"You won't?" Ben might have believed it, if it weren't for how tightly Pete was holding on to him.

"You'll have to fend for yourself," Pete teased. "I'll hide your slippers and douse you with cold water and when you're feeling your very worst, I'll… I'll poke you with sharp sticks or something."

Ben laughed. "You idiot."

"Of course I'll take care of you, Ben. Of course, I will."

* * *

BEN WAS AT WORK IN the back room of his shop—humming along with his new radio—when he heard the front doorbell jingle.

"Ben?" A man's voice called.

Timothy. Pete's older brother. They'd seen each other several times since Pete left—gone to dinner, seen a show. It was nice, becoming closer with Pete's family.

"Benjamin! Are you here?" Timothy's voice was breathless—with laughter, probably, Ben thought.

"Back here, Tim!" Ben called. He added just one more flourish to the skirt he was designing before spinning around. "It's so nice of you to drop—"

"Tim? Tim? Is something wrong?"

Timothy's face was ashen. He was out of breath and couldn't seem to swallow properly.

"Tim? Tim? Is something wrong?"

"Mother—" he panted. "Mother just received—telegram."

Cold rushed over Ben's body. He reached out to hold onto the table behind him.

"Peter's plane's gone down." Ben wasn't hearing this. He wasn't. He wasn't hearing this. He sat down heavily, staring with wide eyes at Pete's older brother.

"His plane's gone down. Pete's reported as missing in action."

CHAPTER FIVE

BEN DREADED WAKING UP EVERY morning. Every night, after he'd fretted and worried and cried himself to sleep, he'd dream of Pete: Pete, leaning to kiss him; Pete, laughing with that funny nose wrinkle; Pete, running down the beach toward him; Pete, in their tiny kitchen, practicing flipping omelets; Pete, happy, alive and whole.

Of course, there were the nightmares: Pete, lost at sea, swimming, swimming, swimming toward a shore that never appeared, then sinking exhausted beneath the waves; Pete, still strapped in his seat, screaming in agony as the flames consumed the plane around him; Pete, captured and tortured; Pete, dead.

The nightmares were easier to deal with. He woke from them quickly, screaming, and would hear Bets sprinting down the hall from "Peter's room" toward him. She would help him, bring him a drink—most often water, but sometimes whiskey—and would sit with him, talking uncharacteristically quietly about silly little things until he fell asleep again.

No, the nightmares were easy. It was harder to wake from the good dreams.

Waking from a happy dream, certain that he'd reach out and feel Pete next to him in their bed, tousled and sleepy-eyed and smiling; Pete warm and safe and sure, always ready to curl himself into Ben's arms, always ready with a kiss and an adorably garbled sleepy mumble and then feeling a cold pillow, Ben would remember—*Pete's shipped out.* But it's okay. He's safe. Then he'd come fully awake and be struck with the chilling realization.

No, Pete wasn't safe. No one knew where he was, if he was alive or d—or injured.

* * *

BEN BECAME ACQUAINTED WITH A different kind of waiting.

Before, he'd waited for Pete with a tumbling agitated turmoil, expecting a letter from him, knowing he was danger, but every day feeling his presence in the world. Pete was somewhere in the world, looking up at the same sky, and there were times Ben would close his eyes and swear he could touch Pete with his mind.

Now, he waited encased in cold, tight numbness. He couldn't feel Pete, not anywhere, and it terrified him. He felt chilled all the time, his hands shaking continually. He didn't want to believe that Pete was dead; he didn't want to accept it, but he tried to make himself remember that might be the case. He thought it would be easier to wait for the worst. Because he thought he might die, as well, if he spent this time stubbornly convincing himself that Pete was coming back, only to have him ripped away again in one crushing final blow.

He couldn't bear to leave the house. What if he missed a telephone call or a telegram? He couldn't bear the idea of missing any news of Pete. He closed the tailor shop. Bets came to stay with him. She phoned the Black Cat to let them know he wouldn't be performing and his clients to inform them there would be a delay in getting their garments. He didn't know what she'd told them, but not a single one complained. Mrs. Horowitz sent him a bouquet of flowers.

"Those are lovely," he said to Bets, automatically. "Will you put them in some water?"

She arranged them carefully in a vase on the mantel, but she was sure he hadn't even seen them.

* * *

Timothy phoned once a day, like clockwork, with updates from his parents—always the same. "No news."

Ben would numbly place the phone's receiver back in the cradle and dully turn to sit on the couch again. Crossing his legs, leaning his elbow on the arm, he'd press the backs of his fingertips under his chin—holding it steady—and return to blindly staring out the window.

Brittle, Bets thought. *He looks brittle.* And she didn't know when and she didn't know how, but she prayed that someone would be there for him when he shattered.

* * *

A letter arrived for Ben—addressed to B. Williams in strange handwriting.

Bets brought it to him at the lunch table. She saw the first spark of interest flash in his eyes as he read the return address.

"It's from—" Ben had to clear his throat. "It's from Charlie. That's Pete's bombardier. Oh my God, Bets, someone survived."

His hands were shaking so badly he couldn't open the envelope. Bets took it from him, slicing the thin paper with a knife.

> *Dear B,*
>
> *I'm writing you this letter because Petey made me promise one night that I'd send a letter to this address if anything ever happened to him.*
>
> *Pete's a swell captain—a swell guy. He always has a smile on his face. He always makes us feel like we could come to him with anything—he is always there for his crew. He always puts us first, and makes sure that we got what we'd earned and that we're taken care of. Not just his flight crew, either—the ground crew for our plane adores him—and the other crews, too. And pretty much the entire base—he just has this way of finding the best in people and showing it to them.*
>
> *I can't tell you exactly what went on during that flight—it'll never get past the censors, but I just want to say please don't give up hope that Pete will be found. We sure as hell haven't.*

We'd been in a pretty bad fight—lots of flak, lots of enemy planes. Our fighters were doing their best to keep them off us, but we took several hits. One engine got shot out on the way there and on the way back—

* * *

"ENGINE TWO IS OUT," JIM reported calmly.

"Roger. Well, this is about to get a lot more interesting." Pete grimaced at the controls in front of him, straining to keep the stick steady. "Keep me updated on fuel status."

"Roger that. Will do."

The sound around them was deafening. He could hear the rattle of their tail gun, the cracking reports of the side guns, Bill's voice over the radio calmly reporting what was going on.

"Engine three is out." Jim's voice was tight.

"Roger."

Pete flipped the switch on his microphone to talk to everyone on his crew.

"Okay, boys. We're down to one engine. I'm not sure how long we can fly on one engine, so I want everyone out of their flak jackets and clipped into their 'chutes now. Make sure everything's secure in case we need to ditch."

The tense minutes wore on.

"Engine one is overheating and on fire."

"Okay, boys, this is it. We're going to ride it out a little farther into the drink, then we're all going to jump." Pete could hear Bill calmly relaying their need to abandon the plane, calling for rescue crews to standby.

One by one, but faster than he thought possible, Pete saw the men of his crew jump, their parachutes popping open and buffeting in the strong wind. Jim unhooked himself from his seat and stood to go towards the open doors. He laid a hand on Pete's shoulder.

"You're coming too, right, Pete?"

Pete nodded. "I'm going to steer this thing out away from us, then I'll be right behind you."

Jim walked back to the open door at the waist of the plane, where the wind was screeching by. He took a second to look back at Pete, who was speaking urgently into the radio, repeating the precise coordinates for the rescuers. Then Jim turned and jumped.

When Jim finally found the rest of the crew in the inky darkness, Charlie was frantically sawing the lines of Bill's parachute, which was filling with water and threatening to drag him down. Jim could barely catch his breath. The other men were treading water, looking miserable but alive. It was cold, bitterly cold, and raining.

They heard the remaining engine groan loudly as Pete veered the huge plane away from them. Then it cut out.

There was a deafening silence.

They heard a loud crack, then a huge fireball lit the night sky as their plane exploded.

* * *

But I swear, B, whoever you are, I swear on the lives of my girl and our future children and anything else you want me to swear on—
I swear I saw a parachute open before the crash.

CHAPTER SIX

PETE WAS ALIVE. AT THE moment, that was about all he could say for himself. He floated on his back, somewhere near where the English Channel bleeds into the North Sea, hoping and praying that he'd been swimming in the right direction.

He'd made it out of the plane in time, got his parachute opened—and no, that hadn't been anything like in training; it had been fucking scary. He hadn't had enough elevation when he had opened it, so it seemed it barely slowed him before he slammed into the water. He'd gotten turned around and tangled, but had managed to find the release latches before the 'chute dragged him down to the bottom. He'd broken the surface just in time to see the orange fireball that used to be his plane. God, he'd felt the explosion through the water.

He'd tried to catch his breath enough to start swimming. He had needed to keep moving—the water had been too cold not to keep moving. *Keep moving, Montgomery. Move your legs. Move your arms.*

The sun was about to break over the horizon—then he'd have a better idea of the direction he should go.

But for now, he lay on his back, resting, arms and legs moving automatically while his life jacket kept his head above water. He noticed that the sky was becoming the exact color of Ben's eyes—bright blue with just a hint of gray

Ben. Benjamin's waiting for him. Benjamin.

He rolled to his stomach and determinedly started to swim.

There was no sign of his crew. He prayed to anyone who would listen that they had been picked up and were already back at base—wrapped in blankets, drinking hot tea and flirting with the nurses.

His plan was to use the sun to keep himself heading roughly north and west. He hoped he'd see something, anything that would let him know he was heading in the right direction.

For now, his goal was to keep his head above water.

His watch was still working, he thought. He couldn't believe it'd been seven hours already. His rest breaks were getting more frequent. His shoulders ached. He had a pain in his side. He couldn't see land. He couldn't see anything except more water. *I'm so tired. I'm going to die out here.*

He rolled to his back to rest again. He was just so tired. All he wanted right now was to lie down and never get up. He wanted to lie down in his bed—their bed—pull Ben down next to him, bury his face in Ben's chest and sleep for days.

Ben.

Pete's eyes snapped open. *Ben.*

You fight, Montgomery. You fucking fight right now. Don't you fucking give up. Fight, Montgomery.

You are not going to leave him alone. You are not going to leave him. You promised. You promised him. You promised. Fight.

Ben. Ben, Ben, Ben

Pete wearily rolled back onto his stomach and started to swim, slowly, timing his movements.

Left arm: *Ben, Ben, Ben*

Right arm: *Ben, Ben, Ben*

Breath: *Benjamin, Benjamin*

Left arm: *Ben, Ben, Ben*

By the time he thought he saw the smudge of shore on the horizon, Pete was dangerously exhausted. The sharp pain in his side was getting worse. Waves kept breaking over his face. He choked. He forgot to breathe.

Nooooooo. No. He lifted his face out of the water. *Ben.*

Pete's face hurt, especially his nose. Something tapped his head. His lips were sticky and whatever the hell was tapping would not stop.

He opened his eyes slowly. He was on shore. He was alive. There was solid ground underneath him. *I am never going swimming ever again in my entire life.*

The tapping was the edge of the waves rolling him gently against a giant piece of driftwood. At least he was out of the sun, already high in the sky again. He had no idea how long he'd been on dry land. But while he didn't think this qualified as comfortable, he was so tired he didn't care.

His nose. Well, he thought there might be a rock in his nose. When he could feel his arms again, he would reach up to investigate.

A few minutes later, he blew his nose forcefully and was rewarded with a torrent of seawater and slime and sludge. And a very small rock. Ha! He was right.

Oh God, wait until Ben hears about this. He's going to laugh at me. I can't wait.

* * *

PETE WOKE UP WHEN HE realized his legs were wet again. He'd been dreaming he and Ben were in bed and he came awake a little panicked, worried he'd just wet the bed.

No. It was the high tide coming in again. *Move, Montgomery.*

He couldn't decide which hurt worse, his head or his throat, and this distracted him from the pain in his body as he hauled himself further up the shore.

Mines. Oh God. What if there are mines? He stopped short, considering. He was not exactly sure where he was *oh please God, let this be England* but he didn't see any barbed wire or any other defensive structures. He closed his eyes and hoped that there were no mines buried in the sand.

The movement jarred whatever wound he had in his side. He put one hand to it, hissing at the saltwater stinging it. It was clearly a puncture wound, and he hoped there was no shrapnel left inside. His flight suit was dark and stiff with blood around it. He hoped he hadn't lost too much blood. His throat was raw, his nose was bleeding, his eyes felt as if they were filled with sand—they probably were. He was so fucking thirsty. He collapsed in the shade of more driftwood and prayed he was higher than the tide line. He was getting so fucking cold. *Oh God, Ben.*

* * *

GINGER WAS JUST WALKING ONTO her ward to report for duty when she saw a farm truck barrel into the compound and stop just in front of the hospital.

A man jumped out and grabbed her arm. "I've got a wounded soldier in the back here. I don't know how badly he's hurt, but he looks like he's been out on the beach for days."

"Wounded soldier?" She let herself be dragged to the bed of the truck. Ginger saw someone curled on his side, facing away from her: a faded uniform, dark hair crusted with saltwater above a severely sunburned neck.

A chill ran through her as she vaulted into the truck. She gently rolled him so she could see his face.

"Peter!"

* * *

THEY HAD HIM STRAPPED TO some sort of bed and were rushing around him. He couldn't remember why everyone seemed so worried. He kept seeing a familiar face topped with a white cap—*I should know that face; she's looking at me with such love in her eyes—who the hell is she?*

Her eyes were blue, not the right blue. He wanted to see blue eyes. Blue eyes with long lashes above kissable lips and—

"Peter, honey?" The woman was holding his hand now, looking into his eyes. "We're giving you some medicine now. You'll feel better in a few minutes."

Her hand was wrong, too. Too delicate. Too small.

"The doctor's going to examine you now. Some of this might hurt, okay, but I promise, it'll be quick."

Pete was too tired to care. He wanted the pain in his side to stop; he wanted the ache in his throat to stop; he wanted everyone to stop talking so he could get back to that nice dream—the one about the bed and the strong hands—

Voices murmured above him. He heard "surgery," "fever," "possible sepsis," "hypothermia." He wasn't sure what any of it meant, but the chills were finally gone, and the pain was going away. He was floating away. But he couldn't. He needed to—

That woman—red hair, red, red—Ginger. Her name was Ginger, he thought—she was still holding his hand firmly. She wouldn't let him float away.

"No, Peter, I promise, I won't let you float away." *Oh, that must have been out loud.* "You're staying right here with me. Okay? Stay with me, Pete."

He heard a panicked voice say, "Hemorrhage." He really wanted to go back to the dream—strong hands and broad shoulders and narrow hips and—Ben. He wanted Ben.

"Peter! You stay with me, honey, okay?" Ginger still held his hand, but she was moving the rest of her. "Pete, there are a lot of people at home who are waiting to hear from you. You stay with me."

He opened his eyes and tried to smile at her. She was behind his head, pulling his hand up near his face, still holding it tightly.

"Pete, the doctor needs to patch you up a bit. This medicine will help you sleep through it— You just breathe deep, now, okay honey? Everything's going to be all right." She lowered a white mask over his face.

She leaned down and whispered in his ear. "Benny needs you. Stay with me."

He breathed deep and dreamed of him.

* * *

BEN SAT AT THE TABLE, his uneaten breakfast in front of him. Bets peeled him an orange, trying to tempt him to eat. She was not certain how much longer he could last like this—barely eating, not sleeping, walking around in a haze.

Last week, she'd woken in the middle of the night to find Ben in bed beside her. He'd turned his head when he'd realized she was awake and grabbed her, holding her fiercely.

He sobbed into her hair.

"I can't stop thinking about him. Every second, every single second, I think about him. I wonder where he is, if he's alive, if he's dead, if he's hurt, if he's okay. Is he in enemy territory? Is he being tortured? Is he alive? Is he all right? Is he okay? Where is he?

"It's constant. I can't think of anything else. I can't even remember to breathe sometimes. Oh God, I miss him so much! I want to hold him and kiss him and just listen to him breathe. Is that too much to ask? I need to hear him breathe. I need him. I want—I need Peter. I just want him back; please God, let me have him back. I can't take this. I can't take not having him; please God, let me have him back. I'll do anything. Please let me have him back."

Bets had run her fingers through his thick hair, not able to find any words of comfort. She just cried along with him. He finally sobbed himself to sleep, his head on her chest, arms wrapped around her tightly.

After that one episode, he slipped back into his shell. She supposed it was easier to feel *nothing*, let *nothing* in, than to feel *everything*.

The doorbell rang. Ben didn't flinch. She put the peeled orange in front of him, wiped her fingers on her napkin and went to answer it.

She came flying back, a thin yellow envelope fluttering in her hands. "Ben. It's a telegram."

He stood up, knocking his chair over. He tore open the envelope, ripping the paper inside nearly in half. With shaking fingers, he held the paper together.

Peter's alive & with me. Recovering well. Letters to follow. Ginger.

He held it out to Bets, let out a huge gust of breath and crumpled to the floor.

A short while later, Bets had him sitting on the floor, next to the desk. She insisted that if he fainted again, he should be as close to the ground as possible. The look he gave her was so full of love and joy and happiness and bubbles of light, she thought he didn't have the heart to argue with her.

She watched his shaking fingers dial Pete's parents' phone number slowly and carefully—tick, tick, tick, hissssssss as the wheel spun back, tick, tick, tick, tick, tick, hisssssssss.

When Pete's mother got on the phone, Bets worried that he wouldn't be able to get the words out. He stumbled over it, interrupting himself, but finally got it across. "Pete is alive, he's in the hospital but recovering. Ginger is sending a letter explaining—we'll know everything soon."

He and Pete's mother cried together, until Bets gently took the receiver.

* * *

Dear B—

I love you.

Now that the most important part is out of the way— Everything's all right. It was rough going there for a while, but I'm going to be okay. I'm stuck in this stupid hospital for a bit longer, while I heal up—nothing too serious. I'm going to be fine.

Ginger's taking good care of me—the rest of the nurses, too. I hate the fucking doctor, because he's the one who keeps saying I can't get out of bed yet—I told him so, but he just laughed and said he gets told that a lot. Ginger says I'm not very convincing when I tell people I hate them.

I love you I love you I love you. I want you to know you saved me, once again. It was only thinking of you that kept me going and got me through. I couldn't bear the thought of leaving you. Only you, my love.

I love you. Have I mentioned that recently? I'm never going to be able to tell you that enough.

I'll write more soon, I promise.

All my love, always.

P.

Ben ran his fingers over the page. The letters were feeble and shaky, not Pete's usual bold penmanship. But it was unmistakably Pete's writing. Pete was sitting somewhere right this very instant, inhaling and exhaling and being alive. Ben was happy.

Ginger's letter contained more details. Pete's condition was still "of concern," but not serious enough to send him home. A real moment of danger, but he was already healing quickly. Desperate for bomber pilots, they'd patch him up, wait for him to heal, then he'd be back on the flight line with the rest of his crew, who were being temporarily shuffled amongst other planes and duties.

Ben wanted Pete home more than anything. He wanted to feel him with his own two hands to know he was okay. But he knew Pete. Knew that Pete would insist on staying with his crew, would never leave them. He understood.

For now, he'd go back to waiting for Pete. And planning. And hoping. The future was uncertain, but, once more, looked very bright.

CHAPTER SEVEN

"That's it, Benjamin." Bets pulled the blanket off him, curled up on the couch. "Put the book down. Comb your hair. We're going out."

"Hey, give that back." Ben snatched at the blanket. "It's raining and cold and no. The only place I am going is into the kitchen for another glass of warm milk."

"Benny," Bets warned. "Benjamin. You can't just sit here all the time. You haven't been back to the Black Cat. When's the last time you went somewhere that wasn't your shop or the grocer's?"

Ben thought. It had been a while. His pause was enough confirmation for Bets.

"Exactly, Benjamin. We're going out."

"I don't want to."

"I don't care. Wash your face; comb your hair; put on something respectable. We leave in exactly seven minutes."

Six-and-a-half minutes later, Ben was shrugging into his trench coat. As they stepped outside the apartment building, he turned up the collar against the chill wind spattering the raindrops.

"Where are we going?"

"The newest USO canteen. My friend works there. She said they're desperate for volunteers. The fleet's in, and they're short-handed."

"The fleet's in?" Ben seemed baffled.

"You'll find out when you get there. For now, all you need to know is it's the perfect solution for us. The fleet's in—you need to get out and I need to get laid."

"Elizabeth Ann McCaffrey!" Ben wasn't really shocked, but he liked to pretend.

"Well, it's the truth." She sniffed and put her arm through Ben's and marched them off down the street.

THE CANTEEN WAS, INDEED, LOOKING for volunteers. They needed young women to act as hostesses, whose job was to chat and dance and laugh and make the soldiers feel relaxed and "at home." They also needed people to run behind-the-scenes to keep the bars and food restocked. Even with Ben's bad knee, they were happy to have him.

He went every night the fleet was in—skirting his way around the crowded dance floor with cases of soda pop, hauling up a giant tray of doughnuts, figuring out how to fix broken coffeepots.

After the first few weeks, he couldn't help himself—he still went back, at all hours of the day, even when it was clear they were no longer short-handed. For the first time since Pete left, he wasn't having trouble falling asleep—he was too exhausted to fret.

Mikey was the only other male volunteer at the canteen. He'd had scarlet fever a few months before, and the doctors said his heart still wasn't strong enough to ship out. He was itching to go and relished the chance to help the war effort. He and Ben challenged each other to see how fast they could mix a drink, how many doughnuts they could steal from Mrs. Jakobsen's kitchen downstairs before she caught them.

It had all started with a joke about Ben being an old man, and had soon spiraled into a fierce but friendly competition between Mikey and Ben. They had agreed that whoever went to the stock room for supplies had to come back in one trip, no matter what they were carrying or risk being mercilessly teased. Both were determined to never to give in, much to the exasperation and laughter of the rest of the regular volunteers.

Ben was in the basement stock room, stacking several crates of soda pop to restock the canteen's bar. It was dark and musty, and he was in a hurry to be upstairs.

"Hey, Benny?" Mikey hollered down the stairs. "Could you bring up a couple of extra tablecloths? They're running short of clean ones up here."

Ben searched the shelves, finally finding a cardboard box containing the last three tablecloths.

"Oh, and Benny?" Mikey called again. "We need another rack of glasses. That clumsy corporal from Kentucky just knocked over a whole shelf of 'em. Maybe bring two of 'em up."

Ben stacked the two boxes of glasses on top of the three crates of soda, thumped the tablecloths down on top and, picking them up, started for the stairs.

"Williams!" Mikey hollered. "Mrs. Mead wants to know if we have any more yo-yos down there, and if we do, can you bring 'em upstairs on the double."

Ben set down the pile of supplies, and began poking through the shelves once again.

"Benny! Are you still down there? Do we have any yo-yos or not?"

"Michael, hold your horses," Ben bellowed sternly. "I'm looking for them."

"Well, you're takin' forever, so I just thought I'd check to make sure you're still alive."

Ben found seven yo-yos stacked on the shelf. He had no idea why there were yo-yos, but Mrs. Mead, one of the canteen's coordinators, wanted them, and Mrs. Mead was going to get them.

"There're seven yo-yos," Ben yelled up.

"Ok, bring 'em on up, please. And while you're at it, we need more stationery for letters. Don't forget the envelopes this time."

"Stationery, don't forget the envelopes," Ben muttered as he stacked and restacked his growing pile of supplies. It was unwieldy, and he briefly considered making more than one trip up the stairs with it all. But he knew if Mikey found out, he'd get teased about being an old man.

"Wait! One more thing!" Mikey shouted. "We need three chair cushions, a box of pencils, and Reverend Martin wants at least four more Bibles."

Ben quickly found the remaining items, rearranging everything so everything might stay put on the way up the stairs.

"Get a move on, Williams!" Mikey yelled. "On the double!"

"I swear to God, Michael," Ben said quietly as he gritted his teeth and slowly climbed up the stairs. "You are such a pain the ass."

"And watch your language."

Ben finally struggled up the stairs, stubbornly carrying his awkward mountain of supplies, barely able to see over it all.

"Okay, Mikey, are you going to help me get this out there?"

"Nah. They don't really need it all right now. I just wanted to see how much you could carry before you went nuts."

"Michael!"

"Hey, they'll need it sometime tonight!" Mikey yelped. "It wasn't all a waste of time!"

"It's heavy!" Ben shouted.

"Oh, come here, you big baby." Mikey reached out and took half of the burden.

It was all worth it when, a few days later, Mikey struggled up the steps carrying three fake Christmas trees, white plastic branches poking him under either arm, an aluminum reindeer balanced on his shoulder, a Santa Claus hat perched on his head, loops of silvered garland hung from his neck and the handle of a basket full of wine glasses precariously held between his teeth.

Ben howled with laughter when he took the basket from Mikey.

"What do you mean we're not decorating for Christmas today?" Mikey had wailed.

* * *

The rest of the volunteers were young women, who quickly found that Ben had a good heart and a sympathetic ear. They also learned of his talent with a needle and put it to good use. At first, he only repaired torn hems from overly exuberant dancing. Then, he helped mend Di's winter coat—now it would last another season. He found himself doing emergency fittings for a soldier who was set to ship out the next day, whose uniforms had just arrived. He brought in an extra sewing machine, just to have one handy.

Di rushed up to him as he walked in the canteen one morning a few weeks later, her blond curls bouncing.

"Anne's getting married. Today. Johnny's just arrived on leave, and he's got the license and the ring and all she needs is a dress," Di babbled, her round face is flushed with excitement. "Can you help?"

Ben shucked off his coat and draped it over a chair. "Of course, I will."

"Oh good. She's been telling me about Johnny, and he seems like such a nice guy, and I just think the world of her, and I've already asked Mrs. Jakobsen if she'll make them a cake and Mikey's taking care of getting them a honeymoon suite and—"

"Di," Ben interrupted. "We need to focus. Are you going to be able to help me?"

"Oh God no," Di laughed. "I can't sew a straight line to save my life— my mother says I'm just a flibbertigibbet. I'm in charge of decorations, and then I thought of finding you and asking if you'll do the dress, because you did such a beautiful job on my coat and it seemed such a shame if Anne couldn't have a proper wedding gown when she's—"

"Di, honey," Ben interrupted again. Di was a sweetheart, a very nice girl, but she'd talk his ear off if he let her. "Has Brenda or Linda come in yet?"

"Oh, they'd be perfect to help you with the dress." Di smiled genially. "Yes, they both just walked in the door."

"Okay, then. You skedaddle and do the decorations, and I'll round up my helpers and get started."

"Isn't this exciting?" she crowed to no one in particular as she scurried off toward the supply closet.

Mrs. Jakobsen, the round and jolly cook and de facto supply master, gave him permission to filch several of the canteen's tablecloths and napkins, which were sparkling white and bleached into softness. He cut into them fearlessly, slicing some into panels for structure, some on the bias for drape. He directed Brenda and Linda where to baste and where to seam. In an hour or two, they coaxed Anne into it, all of them trembling with nerves and emotion, in order to fit it perfectly to her tiny frame. Bets arrived with a beautiful lace-edged hanky for a headpiece, and Di came flying back with a lovely arrangement of silk flowers gleaned from the canteen's table centerpieces.

Anne walked slowly and gracefully down the aisle through the rows of hastily arranged chairs. Her groom, Johnny, bit his lip and grinned when he saw her, a bright flush burning high in his cheeks. Ben didn't realize he was crying himself until he saw Johnny hastily dashing tears from his eyes.

Watching them, Ben felt again the terrible longing, the ache he couldn't ease—missing his own love, the man who looked at him with the same earnest devotion he saw in Anne and Johnny's eyes as they looked at each other. Usually, he carried it with him every minute of every day, sometimes a heavy millstone around his neck, sometimes a cage keeping his heart from beating properly. With a sharp twist of his stomach, he realized he hadn't thought of Pete for several hours. He felt nauseous.

It weighed on him, this waiting. He itched to do something, to go somewhere else, be somewhere else. He wanted to get through his day without the throb in his chest at Pete's empty chair at the breakfast table, the dull twinge in his heart coming home to a silent and empty apartment. He was busy. Most days, he was content—not happy, not exuberant. No longer plunged into the depths of despair, but still with a sharp ache in his chest whenever he caught himself *not* thinking of Pete. And he had caught himself *not* thinking of him several times this week, and the guilt of it felt as if he'd swallowed nails.

But then, there was Anne, standing gravely in front of the hastily arranged altar, one hand held tightly in Johnny's. Her face was so trusting, so grave and certain, Ben was overwhelmed with an anxious craving to see that look on Pete's face again.

* * *

HE REMEMBERED IT WAS A wild winter night, a year or so after they'd met. They'd had dinner with friends, left early and raced through the driving snow back to Pete's apartment, only to find the radiators were malfunctioning. The apartment was cold, but with the blizzard getting worse, they made the decision to wait it out there.

"I know I've got another eiderdown somewhere here." Pete's voice was muffled as he rummaged in his linen closet, pulling out extra blankets. "Here, take these."

Ben laughed as Pete piled his arms high with wool blankets. "Baby, I don't think we're going to need three wool blankets *and* an eiderdown."

"It's freezing cold in here and it's only going to get worse." Pete steered him down the hall towards the living room. "I don't know how much wood is left, but we can build a fire in the fireplace."

The fire built, they huddled together in the blankets for warmth, laughed as they talked over their dessert, then subsided into silence, watching the fire dance and crackle.

"You know—" Pete began, then stopped.

"Hmm?" Ben leaned back against him.

"I—there's—" Pete sounded nervous. "I hope you know there's no one I'd rather be stuck in a snowstorm with, than you."

Ben chuckled. "Well, there's no one I'd rather be stuck in a snowstorm with than you, either."

"I—What would you say—" Pete stammered. "Wait, here. Turn around so I can see you."

Ben sat up a bit straighter, leaning so he could see Pete, who busied himself re-tucking the blankets around them.

"Are you ok?" Ben asked.

"Yeah. I'm fine. I'm—" Pete shook his head, ruefully. "I'm more than fine."

Ben smiled brightly. "You're jumpy."

"I know. I—what would you say if I asked you to move in here? With me?"

Ben hadn't been expecting this, couldn't help grinning. "But—?"

"Wait, before you say anything, let me just—" Pete's face was suffused with excitement. "You know, I thought about having a whole list of why it just made complete sense for you to move in here, financially and how things would just be easier, but—"

"But?" Ben encouraged.

"That's not very romantic." Pete smiled at him, emotion bubbling just below the surface. "And it's not really what I wanted to say."

"It's not?"

"No." Pete stalled for one last moment, then it all came spilling out of him. "What I wanted to say was—please come live here with me. I want you here all the time, every day and every night, and when you're not here, I can't help feeling that it's not really home. It's not really home without you, Ben. I want to see you every minute of every day, when you're cranky because the coffee hasn't been made yet, and when you're mad because I never put my socks in the hamper, and when you've got a stomachache and you're miserable. And when you're excited about something, and you glow, and you're just so fucking beautiful, Benny. I just... I want you. All the time, and for the rest of my life. Just stay with me, live here with me. Please, Ben."

Ben nodded, then kissed him, and the rest of the evening passed without further conversation.

* * *

Anne's face was gravely radiant as she quietly repeated her vows; her eyes glowed with love and hope and trust. Johnny's face was a wondering amazement, as if he couldn't quite believe he was getting his heart's desire.

Pete had had that look, too, the evening they'd finally finished moving Ben's suitcases and boxes and furniture into the apartment on Gramercy Park. Their apartment. Their home.

Ben knew that, no matter what, the hurt of waiting for Pete was nothing compared to the hurt of not having him at all.

* * *

Dear B—

I love you so very, very much. I'm so happy to hear that you're getting out of the house. Those USO canteens sound amazing, and when my leave comes up, I'll be very, very excited if I get to go to one and you're there.

That wedding sounds wonderful, but if you were involved, of course it must have been.

Please don't feel guilty that you're not constantly thinking of me—sweetheart, that's just crazy talk. I know you're not ignoring me. I know you're not forgetting me. You can't think about me all the time or else you're going to go crazy. You're never going to get anything done. I'm in your heart, as you are in mine. No amount of thinking or not-thinking is going to change that.

I can't think about you all the time, either. Aside from being woefully distracting, and damned inconvenient at times because there's very little privacy in the barracks—if you catch my drift—there are times when I just have to Not Think about you. I can't fly a plane if I'm thinking of you. I can't concentrate when I think of you, and your eyes and your lips and your legs—

There I go again. Damned inconvenient, darling. It's currently damned inconvenient how gorgeous you are.

Things here are going well. I got the "all clear" from the doctors yesterday—I'm cleared to return to flying. The crew threw me a small party last night at the mess hall—one of the nurses snuck into the kitchen in the middle of the night to bake a cake—and we're expecting orders any day now. We're just waiting right now.

Please give Bets my love. Ginger sends hers as well—you should be getting a letter from her sometime soon.

I'll write again tomorrow. I love you.

All my love, always.

Your P—

* * *

DAYS WENT BY AND STILL they had no orders. The crew of the Riveting Redhead was back together, and getting restless. Bomber crews lived in a state of near-constant trepidation. To keep their minds off the dangers surrounding them, Pete tried to keep them busy. He organized football matches between them and the other crews. They did morning calisthenics together, egging each other on, challenging and laughing all at once.

No one could understand how he inspired it, but Pete's crew were devoted to each other. Other crews grew fractious with the delays, became short-tempered and quick to fight. Not Pete's crew. They joked and teased like brothers, making no differentiation between officers and enlisted men. They all had their duties throughout the day, but Jim and the waist gunners were often to be found with the ground crew, helping them wash the glass of the nose cone and turrets. Johnny, the tail gunner, would help Bill organize and roll his charts. Their superior officers were in awe, and talked of promoting Pete away from the flight line. He wasn't sure he could refuse a promotion, but he did know he was *not* going to leave his crew.

One night, there was a dance organized—girls were coming from off-base, and the nurses were given special rotating shifts so they could all attend, at least for a short time. Ginger made Pete promise that he'd save her a dance. After completely and utterly charming every single nurse who came to his bedside during his recovery, Pete had gained quite a reputation as a lady's man and was in high demand as a dance partner.

Pete danced. A lot. He made the rounds, finding the girls who hadn't been asked to dance yet, the girls who were too shy until he'd wheedled them out on the floor. He waltzed, he fox-trotted, he jitter-bugged.

Finally, he was tired. He got a drink and sat at a table with several other men and their dates. His copilot, Jim, was sweet on a British girl from a nearby village, and judging from the adoring gazes she was giving him, it was mutual. Glenn sat with a blonde nurse on his lap. She left red lipstick stains as she sucked on his earlobe. He murmured something that made her laugh. He caught Pete's eye, and winked. All around him, people were pairing off, two by two, with roaming eyes and roaming hands and lips, low chuckling and murmurs.

He didn't quite understand it, especially those folks he knew had wives and husbands back home. He wanted Ben, and no one else. Sure, other men caught his eye, a flashing grin or the powerful line of someone's shoulders.

But he could appreciate their attractiveness without ever thinking about acting on it. In truth, he wanted Ben, and only Ben. Only Ben had everything he needed, only Ben held his heart.

Pete leaned back in his chair, a glass in his hand, when Irene, one of his favorite nurses, came over and threw herself onto his lap.

"Helloooooooo, gorgeous," she purred at him, wrapping her arms around his shoulders.

"Hello yourself." He laughed, trying to keep her upright, keeping her skirt arranged for her as she crossed her legs.

"What's a handsome fellow like you doing in a place like this?" she asked, her speech slurred. She must have been spending time outside, sampling bootleg booze.

"Aw, shucks. You think I'm handsome?" She nodded emphatically.

"Well, thank you, honey. I wouldn't be sitting here if you weren't such a good nurse." Pete smiled easily at her.

"I am a good nurse. Are you a good doctor?" Irene giggled.

He laughed. "Well, no, I'm not a doctor, sweetie. I'm a pilot."

"… I know that. I just can't think of anything naughty to say about pilots right now," she admitted.

"That's probably a good thing," he murmured.

"Oh! Are you any good at playing doctor?"

Pete flushed, just a bit. "No, honey. I'm not."

"Petey, will you have a drink with me?" Irene was not going to be deterred.

"Sure, honey, would you like water or ginger ale?"

"Ohhhhh, that's not what I want," she said, wiggling in his lap.

He bent to whisper in her ear. "Irene, you really should get some sleep. You're going to regret this tomorrow morning."

"I know, but I wouldn't have enough courage to ask you this if I were sober," she whispered.

"Ask me what?" *Oh God, what does she have to be drunk to ask me? No matter what it is, this conversation is not going to go well.*

"Come with me." She wobbled to her feet, tugging at his hand.

He glanced around the table. Everyone seemed to be engrossed in their own conversations, giggling and laughing. Only Johnny, sitting next to him, seemed to notice. He looked appalled.

"Okay, honey, okay." Pete let himself be led away from the table.

They got to a quieter corner—Pete carefully steered them away from the dark corners full of couples already canoodling.

Irene wrapped her arms around his waist and took a deep breath.

"What did you want to talk about, honey?" Pete was pretty sure he knew where this was going, but Irene was wonderful, Irene was sweet and kind and good and pretty and if it weren't for one—quite major and ultimately deal-breaking—detail, he was fairly certain he'd be happy about where this conversation was leading.

"Ever since you were on my ward," she slurred, "and I helped give you those sponge baths—" She paused to swallow.

"Ever since then, I just can't stop thinking about you. And how handsome you are. And how nice you are. And dreaming about you and wanting your arms around me. And to kiss…"

"Irene, wait," he interrupted, putting his hands on her shoulders to push her back slightly. "Wait a minute. I… I'm flattered, really. And if things were different, I'd be really happy that you thought that—but, I've got… I've got someone back home."

"Oh." Irene's face fell. "Oh, I see."

"Honey, you're wonderful and fun to be around and cute and all that. I just… I just can't. I'm so sorry."

"Oh God. God, I'm so stupid.

"You're not stupid. You're not stupid—you're wonderful. I'm so sorry I can't… honest, I am. I'm so sorry."

"I'm stupid, because I'm standing here, drunk, in uniform, and telling you that I want you and, oh God." She put her hands over her face. Pete thought she'd started to cry.

"Irene, I… I'm sorry if I gave you the impression that I… that I could. Please don't cry, honey. Don't."

"What's her name?" Irene sniffed.

"Uhhhhhh. Her name?" Pete's thought went blank, in panic. For whatever reason, no one had ever asked—everyone else just took it for granted when he said he had a sweetheart back home. Not a wife, not a girlfriend. "A sweetheart," that worked for them.

Suddenly, Ginger was there, with her arm on Pete's shoulder. "Pete? I do believe you owe me a dance, sugar. Oh, sorry, I didn't see you were. . ."

Pete untangled Irene's arms from around him. "Ginger, can you do me a favor and help Irene back to her barracks? I think she's not feeling very well."

Ginger took it all in in an instant. "Of course. Come on, sugar, let's get you to bed, okay?"

Irene wiped the tears from her eyes and laughed. "Yeah, honey, that'd be swell of you. I'm getting an awful headache."

"You take care, okay, honey?" Pete straightened Irene's uniform jacket.

"Okay, Pete." She smiled at him, weakly. "Thanks for being so nice."

Pete watched as Ginger looped her arms under Irene's gently, holding her up. They walked somewhat unsteadily into the dark, towards the nurse's barracks.

Pete went to the bar and ordered another whiskey. He marched straight to their table, sat in the chair next to Glenn and his gal and sipped it with purpose.

"You okay there, Montgomery?" Glenn managed to tear himself away from the nurse on his lap to glance blearily at his friend.

"You bet. I just needed some air."

"Good." Glenn turned his attention back to the giggling woman.

When Ginger returned a little while later, with a smile and a nod at Pete, the dance was still in full swing. As he laughed and joked with the people at his table, Pete could see another girl, one of the village girls, wobbly weaving her way straight toward him. *Oh God, not again.*

Ginger hopped up from her seat and nearly vaulted into Pete's lap with a loud squeal.

"Whoa there, honey." Pete wrapped his arms snugly around Ginger's waist. "You're going to knock us over."

"Yes, but if I wasn't enthusiastic enough, that girl was going to come over here and ask to switch places with me. As it is, she realizes you're otherwise occupied, and she'll find someone else to target. Oooh! Change of plans and see? Off she goes!" Ginger was pointing.

"Oh, God, Red. Don't point."

"Well, judging from the discussion in the ladies room just a while ago, there are several girls who are going to try to get your attention this evening, so to speak."

"Oh God. What have I done to deserve this?" Pete groaned.

"You're gorgeous. And kind. And charming. And fun. And gorgeous— did I mention how attractive you are?" She leaned back to put her hands on his cheeks and pat them.

"It's not your fault, Petey. You just can't help it," she said, sighing dramatically.

"Things would be easier if I was just an ass? Would that help?"

"Maybe for a while. But sometimes, there's just something about a gorgeous ass—"

Pete nearly choked. "Yeah, there is," he muttered.

Ginger chuckled. "So, I'll be your bodyguard. I'll keep the girls off you, you dance with me and get me drinks and stuff. Just like old times."

"Just like old times." Pete laughed. "Thank God you're here, Red."

She giggled delightedly.

It was nice to have a friend—a friend who *knew.* It was even nice to have someone sitting on his lap, someone to wrap his arms around and have a little snuggle with. There was no way around it, Ginger was a cuddler. They were cuddling, just like old times.

Except, if it really was just like old times, Ben would be walking through the door at any moment, pushing Ginger unceremoniously off Pete's lap, and making some sharp comment about "not a competition" and "do I need to draw you a diagram" or something to make them all laugh.

At the thought of Ben, Pete suddenly felt empty. He wrapped his arms more tightly around Ginger and rested his head against her shoulder.

PETE LEFT THE PARTY A bit later, dizzy with too much whiskey he'd sampled from Glenn's and Ginger's hidden flasks. He wasn't sure whether his head or his heart was aching worse. He stumbled in the dark along the dirt path back to the barracks, swamped with homesickness: for his life back in the States, for the way things used to be, for Ben. He thought he'd find his bed, maybe pull out his photo album and will himself to sleep before he could get too maudlin.

He could still hear the music playing from the dance as he walked in, tripping as he always did at the entry. He and the officers of three other plane crews shared a Nissen hut. The hut was a giant metal tube cut in half lengthwise and set on the ground. The curved metal that formed both the walls and the ceiling had been painted dark green, with heavy blackout curtains hung at the windows on each end. Dark green wool blankets on the beds—more like cots, really—dark green footlockers at the end of each man's bed. Pete swore he would never own anything that shade of green ever again. Pete always found it cold inside; the meager heat of the stove at one end never quite reached the other side. When it rained, the metal roof and walls echoed loudly.

The overhead lights were off, and no one had drawn the blackout curtains. He made his way down the row of beds to his bunk. He'd just get rid of this necktie, shuck off his jacket, throw himself on his bed and not think about anything until reveille sounded tomorrow morning.

Two steps down the row, and he had the cloudy realization he was not alone in the barracks. He hesitated, hoping he hadn't been too noisy and awakened one of his fellow officers. He tip-toed to his bunk, the next one down the line, just a few more steps. He stealthily slipped off his jacket and boots, then winced at the squeak of his mattress.

Once he was lying down with the party music faintly drifting down to him, he was aware of another stealthy sound, this one coming from the other end of the room: high-pitched breathing, with small hitches as if someone were running at top speed, and a rhythmic smacking sound. Pete's ears began to burn when he recognized it.

He was about to roll over with his pillow over his ears when he heard a wet squelching pop, all too familiar—and realized, with a flashing vision of Ben, his lips red and swollen, pinning him to the bed and swallowing him down—there were two people at the other end of the barracks.

He had nowhere to go, no way to give them privacy without further announcing his presence. No, he decided, the most polite thing to do would be to put his pillow over his head, do his best to fall asleep and stay asleep the entire night and, in the morning, play dumb if anyone mentioned any barracks shenanigans.

It was no use. He could hear them through his pillow. The breathing became heavy, the wet slurping loud and lewd. Whoever she was, she sounded talented and eager—no, he couldn't think like that. *No relief this evening, so don't even start, Montgomery.* He closed his eyes as tight as he could, and tried to think of calm, placid, boring places—anything that was the furthest thing from thoughts of Ben and Ben's mouth and—

The breathing stuttered again, then with a keening soft wail, Pete heard: "Oh God, Glenn. Yes, just like that."

There was no mistaking it. The talented and eager mouth belonged to Glenn and whomever he was using it on was most definitely not a woman.

* * *

PETE HAD NO TIME TO wonder about his friend's love life. Bad weather and increased flak made the next few flights hell. As it was, barely half the number of planes were making it back home each time they flew out and difficult flying conditions only made it worse. Many of the returning flight crews joined the ground crews already "sweating out the mission"—waiting on the flight line until their planes and crew came back. Or until it became apparent that they would not.

The Riveting Redhead had been back for quite a while, her crew sprawled quietly on the grass near the airstrip, playing cards and smoking cigarettes. The dark and deadly bombing runs meant hours and hours in the frozen night, the high altitude robbing them of oxygen, draining them of strength and energy. When they returned, they were beyond exhaustion, so tired they couldn't sleep, and so stressed they needed time to begin to relax.

The after-effects of adrenaline were still pounding through Pete's veins, making his head throb and his stomach roll. He lay on his back, staring up at the bright blue sky dawning cloudless and perfect, and thought about the house on the beach, and tried to still his mind. He pictured a picnic on the beach with Ben, dancing in the living room, baking a cake, chopping firewood. He treasured the memory of all the normal, regular, usual things he used to do with Ben. He hoarded them like a miser, turning the memories over in his head, gloating over of the pile of them, cataloging each smile, each wink, each laugh of Ben's that he could remember.

At first, the other planes would come back one right after another, in various states of damage—no one ever seemed to make it back unscathed. Then they came back in waves, then in small groups, and then, the last few would come limping home. Pete could feel the vibration of the planes landing. He kept his eyes glued to the sky without watching them touch the ground: his own personal superstition.

Flying in formation was one of the more dangerous parts of a bombing run. They were crammed in together, strategically placed, each plane's gunners positioned for maximum coverage against enemy planes. The formation had the smaller, more agile and versatile fighter planes buzzing all around them, drawing off fire and doing their best to protect the larger planes. On the bombing run, they were locked in to flying in a straight line—easily plotted by the enemy and easy for the enemy fighters to pick them off like sitting ducks. They were unable to divert, unable to change course and unable to get away.

By the time the Redhead landed, they knew their group had lost four planes, all to enemy fire. But a fifth plane was still unaccounted-for: one of the new crews had lost contact.

Pete had seen the young pilot at their mission briefing the night before. He looked nervous and worried and so lost; he hadn't been at the base for more than a few weeks. Pete remembered his first weeks here. The moments before his own first flight held excitement—excitement to be finally doing what he'd trained for months for, flying for his country, being a hero like in the movies. The moments before the second run out had been filled with terror and dread. He'd survived his first flight, hours and hours in the bitter cold, and he knew exactly what it entailed. He now knew there would be no one to correct his mistakes, no one to give him a second chance, and the enemy planes chasing him wanted him dead.

Pete had wanted to introduce himself on their way in to the briefing, offer some calming words, take him under his wing for a bit. But the pilot had marched straight to the front with such purpose, defying his fear, determined to make it through this second mission. He'd sat with a crease between his eyebrows as he carefully noted down everything the briefing officer had to say. As they'd walked out to the planes, Pete had watched the young man meet the rest of his crew and adjust his heavy shearling flight jacket across his shoulders. They all looked so young, Pete thought. None of them could have been more than twenty years old.

The sun was well up over the horizon now; bright sunshine streamed over the airfield. A light breeze, fresh and green-smelling, stirred the tall grasses at the edge of the airstrip. There was a beautiful day ahead of them.

Pete lay on his back and kept his eyes fixed on the blue sky, listening hard for the low drone of aircraft engines, and hearing only the light twitter of birds and the muted murmurs of his own crew as they decided to pack up and head to the barracks. Pete stayed, hoping against dwindling hope that this young crew might make it back, might have survived whatever it was that made them lose contact, might even now be staggering home to fly another day.

A shadow fell across his eyes as Glenn came into view, peering down at him with a raised eyebrow.

"They're most likely gone, you know," he said calmly. "Even if they were shot down and somehow survived the crash, we all know their chances of surviving on the ground behind enemy lines ain't good. And if they weren't shot down, they don't have enough fuel to be out this long and make it back."

Pete screwed up his lips, blinking furiously against tears that he tried to hold back, and nodded his head.

Glenn lay down next to him on the grass.

"They're just—" Pete began, swallowing hard around the lump in his throat. "They were just so young, you know?"

Glenn sighed heavily. "Yes. I know."

"I don't know their names. I didn't even get a chance to say hello. I didn't take the time to say hello. Which," he sniffed, "is ridiculous, I know, as if me saying hello might have kept them safe? But…"

"They were so young," Glenn finished.

"They didn't get a chance to— They hardly had the chance to—" And now tears were coming, sliding down into Pete's hair. Grief was coming unpacked now; the death of this young crew was the final straw that cracked him open. Grief for all the other crews they'd lost—all men Pete had joked and laughed with; grief for their wounded—many of whom would go home scarred inside and out; grief for the people in the path of the bombs—people just doing their jobs in factories and offices; grief at the loss of his own life as he knew it before. Grief for them all, all irreparably changed.

"The pilot, his name was David." Glenn's voice was thick and halting. "He was twenty years old, from San Francisco. He was a star first baseman on his high school baseball team. He loved Frank Sinatra and dancing."

Pete kept staring up at the sky, letting the tears flow. He could hear the hitch in Glenn's breath and knew his friend was crying, too. He reached out, moving his hand just slightly and felt Glenn's snap to grip his tightly. They grieved together, for all of them.

CHAPTER EIGHT

Dear P—

Congratulations on your promotion! I'm so proud of you. I know how proud you must be, of yourself and of your crew. They sound like a swell group of guys.

I have your portrait framed on my desk, so I can look at you as much as I want—maybe I'll carry it from room to room, just to have you with me. Will they take a new one with your captain's bars?

Bets and I are still volunteering at the canteen, having a wonderful time and meeting all sorts of wonderful people. Mainly, we're just chatting with soldiers, making sure they have enough to eat and that they're having a good time. Bets says she's hoping to "bag a colonel" and I shudder to think of all that that might imply.

Not much else has changed. It's cold here now, and everyone's having the hems rolled on their last season's winter coats, trying to make do without a new one. And so I'm up to my ears in woolens, but at least it keeps me busy.

Bets has just come in and read over my shoulder. She wants me to inform you in no uncertain terms that she is not attempting to wheedle or finagle any colonel into a marriage proposal or otherwise long-term indecent proposal of any sort. In any case, she keeps muttering something about the highest-ranking officer she's met there is a major. I take it to mean she thinks marrying a major won't suffice.

She's a menace and a handful and a riot, all in one. I adore her. But, you already knew that.

I'm sorry for being silly tonight. I'm feeling light as a feather and flippantly silly. We've had so much fun this evening, she and I.

I wish you were here. I miss you so.

All my love, always.

Me.

* * *

BEN WAS IN THE STOCKROOM, loading a tray with soda pop when Mikey came barreling down the staircase.

"Ben! Get your bony ass upstairs!"

"What's wrong?"

"The singer is caught in traffic. The crowd's chomping at the bit, the band's ready, but the bandleader insists they need a singer, so I told them you sing, and they're waiting for you."

"You... what? What?" Ben started to set the tray down.

"Give me the tray, dummy. You go sing." Mikey nudged him roughly toward the stairs.

Mikey had discovered Ben's singing ability one Saturday morning while Ben was taking inventory in the stockroom. Ben had thought he was alone and was singing loudly. He was completely surprised and embarrassed when Mikey began applauding after a particularly raucous rendition of "Why Don't You Do Right?"

Ben stumbled up the stairs and made his way across the crowded dance floor toward the stage. He tripped walking up the steps. The bandleader eyed him critically and snapped, "'Tuxedo Junction,' in A. Now."

Ben went on autopilot. He did love to perform. He knew this song by heart. He wasn't quite as comfortable a showman as Pete, but he did have a certain something special of his own.

The crowd went wild at the end of the song.

"'I've Got a Gal in Kalamazoo,' in E flat," the bandleader snapped again. Ben sang it flawlessly.

It went on splendidly for the next several songs. The crowd loved it— dancing and cheering and having a wonderful time. Each song brought a little bit more respect to the bandleader's voice as he gave Ben the set list.

Then it was time to sing "I'll Be Seeing You." Ben closed his eyes. He let his voice throb, pouring out all the love and longing he felt for Pete into it. When he opened his eyes, his gaze was drawn to the side of the stage. There stood the real singer for tonight: the infamous Gwen Andrews, diva extraordinaire, known for her sexually-charged performances that had gotten her banned from several clubs in Washington. She was scandal-rag fodder—always in and out of love with the wrong men.

Gwen Andrews, standing there in her red satin gown, her hair and makeup done to perfection. Gwen Andrews, who was famous for screaming fits when things didn't go her way, was watching Ben with the strangest look on her face.

"I'm afraid I don't understand, Miss Andrews," Ben stammered, sitting in a quiet booth after the Gwen Andrews Singers show was over. He'd seen her in newsreels and magazines, of course; he was determined not to stammer like a star-struck schoolboy. Up close, he could see that her eyes were green and her red hair was a little sweaty from the enthusiastic performance she'd given. Up close, she looked smaller than in all the pictures and somehow softer.

"It's quite simple, Mr. Williams. My lead tenor and duet partner, Tex, has flown the coop." Gwen paused to sip her highball—vodka, rocks with a twist—and swallowed. "Good riddance, the wretched man. But now I find myself in need of a tenor and it seems the good Lord has seen fit to provide me with one."

With a negligent flick of her fingers, she waved away one of her entourage, who was approaching the table.

"I'm prepared to make it worth your while. You'd be lead tenor; sing a few duets with me. Maybe sing one or two songs on your own, after we see how you do on the road. I'll have my people contact your agent to draw up a contract."

Ben had been nearly knocked flat earlier when he'd been summoned by someone named Vicki—Gwen's assistant/flunkie. Now this bombshell opportunity was being dropped in his lap. Plain as day, here was an opportunity to stake his claim, to regain some of the dignity and self-respect he hadn't wanted to admit he'd lost when he'd received his 4F enlistment rejection. What would it take to leave the city quickly? There was the shop to think about. He hadn't taken in many new pieces after Pete's accident, coasting by on Pete's dividend check that came like clockwork in the mail. He could probably finish those up within a few days, maybe sooner if Bets helped him deliver them. He could ask Bets to keep an eye on the apartment, and maybe Mikey would take the train out with her and help her make sure the cottage was closed up properly. He frowned—maybe he should do that himself, because sending the two of them out to Long Island alone might be asking for trouble.

Ben shook his head and took both a steadying breath and a sip of his own vodka.

"I don't have an agent." He didn't react to Gwen's start of surprise. His eyes never wavered from hers.

"No agent? Well, we'll get you one."

They continued to eye each other.

"Any other problems I should know about?" Gwen asked with one eyebrow raised.

Ben pursed his lips, considering.

"Could be. I'm a homosexual."

She looked at him steadily. "Not the set of pipes I'm interested in."

He choked on his drink.

"I'll be honest with you, Mr. Williams. This tour—this tour is taking a lot out of me and I may need to have the spotlight on someone else from time to time." She grimaced briefly at the damp cocktail napkin she was tapping lightly with her fingertips. "And, it might be a refreshing change. I'm tired of having my ass fondled whenever the boys think I'm not paying enough attention to slap them silly."

"Yes, I think we can guarantee that I will happily leave your ass alone, Miss Andrews."

"Gwen, please."

"Ben." He held out his hand, and they shook.

"Very well, then. Welcome aboard, Ben." Gwen's smile was suddenly warm and friendly. "Now, how about another drink?"

HE RACED HOME DIRECTLY AFTER his meeting with Gwen and pounded on Bets' door.

"This had better be good, Williams," she growled as she answered her door, disheveled in her slippers and robe. "I know you're not going to be able to appease me in the way that most gentlemen who rudely awaken me in the middle of the night—"

"Oh for heaven's sake," he snapped, reaching to grab her hand and drag her along to the elevator and his apartment. "I've got the most fantastic news. I need to pack and I need your help."

* * *

AND JUST LIKE THAT, BEN found himself a singing sensation on tour with one of the decade's most notorious sex-kittens. Working tirelessly, Ben scrambled to finish his tailoring, quickly emptying his shop of all his orders. He wrote Pete to tell him and gave him the new address for his mail, though with overseas mail delivery being what it was, he had no idea where he'd be when Pete got the news. He wrote to his father and his sister. He drove to the cottage to make sure everything was closed up snug and tight. He drew dust drapes across the furniture in their apartment; gave away all the potted plants and, in just over a week, Ben Williams was en route to join the Gwen Andrews Singers tour in Albuquerque, New Mexico. It all seemed like a dream, like a plot from a movie, and he couldn't quite believe it was really happening.

They performed in sleepy little towns to sell war bonds and in larger cities, where they had benefit concerts before heading to the nearest hospital to perform for recently returned soldiers in recovery.

Gwen was snappish, even brusque, with nearly everyone—everyone except Ben, for whatever reason—but with the soldiers, she was sweet and mischievous and flirtatious. At publicity stops, she complained about her feet hurting after barely five minutes. With the soldiers, she never complained. She held their hands. She kissed their cheeks. She made them forget where they were, just for a little while.

At first, Ben had a hard time at the hospitals, though he did his best not to show it. In every injured soldier's face, he saw Pete, and it wrenched his heart. After the first few tour stops, seeing the sorrows lift from people's faces while the group sang and bantered, seeing the weight of life without their loved ones ease just a bit, he felt a sense of purpose. He could help these people with his talents.

In a veteran's hospital near Chicago, a young man with so many injuries Ben couldn't even tally them, lay on his back, staring dully out the window next to his bed. He was in a cast from his mid-thigh to his mid-chest—his bare torso and bare legs poked out at either end. His right arm had been amputated just below the elbow.

"And how are you?" Gwen said brightly as she stopped next to his bed. He didn't turn his head.

She considered him for a minute, then crawled into bed next to him. His head spun toward her—and she smiled impishly at him.

"Hi there, soldier," she purred. "My name's Gwen. What's yours?"

"J… John," he stammered.

"Well, hello, John. It's so lovely to meet you."

He stammered again.

She looked up at him through her eyelashes. "Listen, honey, you just do what those doctors and nurses tell you and you get yourself healed up fast."

She ran her hand over his bare chest, "— and when you get that cast off those hips of yours, you come and see me, sugar."

With a last caress and an audacious wink, she slid seductively off the bed. As she walked away, her hips swinging, Ben looked back to see John, looking flabbergasted and yet somehow hopeful, watching her walk.

Ben followed behind her, smiling at patients and nurses and doctors, desperately trying not to picture how Pete must have looked, lying in agony in a hospital bed like these.

* * *

ANOTHER DAY, ANOTHER HOSPITAL. GWEN, with Ben and the rest of her entourage trailing behind, made her way through the rehabilitation ward, watching wounded soldiers relearn skills for their daily lives, without arms, without legs.

A young freckle-faced soldier with a brand-new artificial leg sat in a wheelchair, staring doubtfully at the set of parallel bars in front of him.

"It's all about motivating this one," a nurse whispered to Gwen. "Physically, he's ready to walk. But he believes he can't."

"What's his name?" Gwen asked.

"Billy."

Gwen nodded, then sauntered over to him. "Billy-boy, could you help a girl out?" Ben could practically hear her batting her eyelashes. "These nurses have been dragging me all over creation this morning, and my feet are worn out."

Ben wasn't sure how talking about her feet hurting to a man who only had one foot left was going to motivate him.

"Do you know where I could find a seat?" She smiled demurely at the dumbstruck young man.

He looked frantically around for a chair—but there wasn't one.

"Uh-oh," Gwen pouted. "I guess I'll just have to share yours." She plopped herself in his lap, wrapping her arms around his shoulder to keep from sliding off.

Ben couldn't hear their whispered conversation—Gwen seemed to be teasing, and Billy was bashful, but eager to keep talking to her.

"Vicki, honey, do we have any of those photos from the Monte Carlo shoot?" Gwen called.

Vicki tucked her black hair behind her ear, searched through the satchel she carried and pulled out a stack of photos. Gwen slid off Billy's lap and began thumbing through them, "Now, no peeking, Billy-boy."

She finally selected one and folded it over three quarters of the way up from the bottom. Ben thought she grinned like a cat as she turned it around so Billy could see that only her smiling head and her tantalizing bare shoulders were visible; the rest of her was hidden beneath the fold.

She walked to the parallel bars, pinning the photo on the wall at the end.

"Now, sugar. If you want to see what I'm wearing in that picture, or what I'm *not* wearing, you're gonna have to walk on over here and get it yourself."

The rest of the soldiers let up a whoop of encouragement. Billy looked flustered, but determined.

"Vicki, you leave the rest of that stack with the nurses. Ladies, whenever you feel inspiration is lagging, you change the picture. You see how to fold it? And the rest of you, I don't want *any of* you spoiling the surprise, you got it?" She pointed fingers at the men, smiling broadly.

"Now, Billy, honey, I have to go. You be a good boy now, for me?" She kissed his cheek soundly and walked away slowly with her signature saunter.

* * *

THE FLAK WAS HEAVY THAT night. Pete could see the small puffs of bright light all around them, like clusters of fireflies on a summer night. The plane shook and rattled as they were forced to fly through the clouds of shrapnel in order to stay on target.

Then, their payload delivered, they flew higher, out of reach of most of the anti-aircraft measures. They still had to fend off the enemy fighter planes, which were bent on harassing them and taking down as many of them as possible, even on their flight home.

Pete was grimly doing his best to stay in formation. Just out his window, just off his left wing, he could see the Queen of Tarts, bleeding fuel.

He could hear the loud reports of the Redhead's machine guns blasting and the frenzied voices of the gunners as they spotted enemy planes as well as Bill's calm tones, relaying information, and Jim's quiet voice, keeping him apprised of the situations around them.

The Redhead seemed to jump a few inches to the right. When Pete looked back, a cloud of black smoke was already dissipating off his left wing. He jolted in surprise, looking quickly for Glenn's plane, and saw her pinwheel out of formation and fall out of the sky, spewing smoke and flames before exploding in a ball of fire.

Teddy, their left waist gunner, chimed in. "Four of them got out. I see two with 'chutes. And two without."

Pete closed his eyes. Nine crewmen had been on the plane, and only two of them had a chance of surviving. He was certain Glenn would have stayed with the hopelessly damaged plane, flying it out and away from the others, ensuring no more lives than necessary were lost.

THEY'D AGREED, ONE AFTERNOON OVER coffee that, if anything were to happen, if they didn't come back from a flight, the other would take the responsibility of cleaning out their footlocker. It was a grim tradition at their base: boxing up personal effects to send home to next-of-kin, distributing to the rest of the guys any goodies that were leftover, disposing of things that weren't important or shouldn't go home to family.

Pete was alone in the barracks. He dragged Glenn's footlocker to the side of Glenn's bunk, then sat down heavily and opened the top slowly. Everything was neatly folded and in its place; inspections here weren't as frequent as at other bases, but they still happened. He mechanically listed off the contents in his head. Spare buttons, shoelaces, a shoe-polishing kit, socks of both winter and summer weight wool would be divvied up among the guys. The cigarettes, candy bars and cough drops, too. Field manuals would be returned to Corporal Johnson for redistribution. Under the heavy top tray were neatly folded rows of underwear, undershirts and a sweater.

Pete was about to replace the tray and put the footlocker back when he paused. There was nothing personal in this box, nothing that would raise any eyebrows, or give an indication of anything about the man who owned it. No letters from home, no photos taped carefully to the lid. Nothing to say, "This was Glenn." Nothing to say his friend had been here. There was nothing left.

He looked around the barracks, empty on a bright and sunny afternoon, and felt lonely. He picked up the sweater and, holding it close, briefly inhaled the scent of Glenn, the faint smell of hair pomade and aftershave. He was startled when a leather-bound notebook fell from its carefully hidden spot in the folds.

He hesitated a moment before untying the leather lacing. If it had been anyone else, he would have never dared, but he could almost feel Glenn's presence. He could picture Glenn's raised eyebrow, hear him saying, "Well, go ahead, Montgomery. Don't be such a ninny."

A few snapshots were tucked in here and there. A battered one of Glenn and a woman who had his laughing eyes, written in pencil on the back "Mama and I." A slightly blurry one of a muscular young man on a beach, hands on his hips, grinning in the sunshine. Written on the back was simply: "Steven." Pete was certain Glenn had never mentioned anyone named Steven.

Glenn's handwriting was scrawling and lackadaisical. He didn't write much, or it seemed, very often. Pete flipped through the pages and found a strip of photo booth snaps, three pictures of Glenn and Steven, arms slung around each other's shoulders. In the first, they both grinned into the camera. In the second, Steven's head was turned toward Glenn's shoulder, almost seeming to rest on it. The third showed Glenn's head just resting on Steven's; both of them had their eyes closed.

It could have been just one of those funny photo booth mistakes—everyone had photos with eyes half-open or mouths open about to speak. It could have been just the two of them moving into a different pose, photographed before they were ready. But Pete was sure it wasn't. Pete was certain this was a tender moment between Glenn and his lover, caught on film.

A well-worn letter, fragile with reading, to Glenn, from Steven.

> *Your mother is doing well. We have lunch after church on Sundays. I think she's really missing your dad, but she's staying busy.*
>
> *Everyone is doing fine. We all miss you. Some of us are having trouble sleeping, but we keep each other's spirits up.*
>
> *We love you, we miss you,*
> *Steven.*

And then, nothing more from Steven. No letters, no photos. No mention of him in the rest of Glenn's journal. In fact, there was nothing more written, just a newspaper clipping of Glenn's mother's funeral notice carefully tucked between the pages, still sharply creased.

But, tucked in the back of the journal, among the fresh pages, he found a couple of newer snapshots: one of Glenn's crew, posed in front of The Queen of Tarts, grinning for all their worth; one of Pete and Ginger outside the mess hall, arm in arm, trying to look very serious and formal, but failing. Pete remembered Ginger's raucous burst of laughter just after it was taken.

And one final recent photo. Glenn and the young pilot, David, arms slung around each other's shoulders, grinning happily into the camera.

Oh.

Oh, Glenn.

* * *

GWEN AND BEN WERE SITTING on an empty stage, somewhere in Kansas, running through some new songs. Gwen was an accomplished pianist, though she never played in public. They were finding what keys worked for which songs to keep them in her range and in Ben's.

"… He's telling her to 'shoo' for crissakes. He's going off to war, and telling her to 'shoo.' Jackass. You should sound lazy. Confident. Indolent… yet supremely sexy. You know, like those guys who are just assholes, but you can't help but want to fuck 'em."

Ben sighed. "Yeah. I sure do."

Gwen snorted. "Yeah, I bet you do, Williams."

They both giggled.

"Do you… Is there someone… do you have a regular…" She looked around furtively, to make they were alone. "Is your… boy… Is he ever like that?"

"Peter." Ben supplied. "His name is Peter. We've been together four years now. And no, he's not usually like that."

"Not *usually.* So he is… *sometimes.*"

Ben laughed shortly. "Yes, on occasion."

"And what happened then?" Her eyes were bright and curious.

* * *

IT WAS A LAZY SATURDAY afternoon spent speculating on the sex lives of certain matinee idols. Pete had Ben in stitches with his mimicry; Ben suggested more and more stars for Pete to try.

Pete's spot-on impersonation of Clark Gable in *Gone with the Wind* had caused a burning in Ben's metaphorical Atlanta. A few moments of ferocious grappling and moaning and then the Yankees were coming, indeed.

After Pete had pulled out of Ben, his eyes gleamed wickedly, infuriatingly gorgeous as he watched his lover continue to gasp and writhe on the bed below him.

"Hey, thanks, baby," Pete growled in his best Humphrey Bogart voice, slapping Ben's bare hip. "Now, go get me a sandwich, would you?"

* * *

"OH MY GOD." GWEN GIGGLED. "And what did you do?"

"Oh, I went to the kitchen and made him a sandwich. Then I brought it back to bed," Ben said matter-of-factly, "where I jerked him hard again. Then I wouldn't let him come *or* eat the sandwich until he'd sucked me off."

"Oh my God." Gwen choked on her drink and coughed until her eyes watered.

"Well, ask a vulgar question, get a vulgar answer. I figure if you're going to fantasize about two men fucking each other, I might as well give you some good material."

"God, you're rude today." Gwen laughed.

"You, too, sweetheart. Now, can we work on the song?"

Gwen stuck her tongue out at him and turned back to the piano. Ben closed his eyes and remembered the appealing arrogance he didn't often show, the confident swagger, the brash sex appeal of Pete. The song went flawlessly.

* * *

THREE DAYS LATER, GWEN BURST into Ben's hotel room. "Pack your bags, Williams. We leave at the end of the week. The USO's come through. We're headed to Europe."

CHAPTER NINE

In Pete's dream, Ben was making eggnog in the kitchen of their apartment.
Pete looked furtively down the hall to the guest room. He gingerly pulled a long, wide box from the paper bag, stepped into "his" closet and deftly slid it into the middle of the tower of boxes on the shelf, where it blended perfectly with the myriad of other boxes Ben kept stored there. *Darling, we are not going to just shove our summer clothes on the shelves here. That's what boxes are made for...*

He'd have to wrap Ben's Christmas present later, maybe when Ben snuck out to Bets' apartment, where he was hiding Pete's presents.

The dream shifted. They were on the beach near their house, running and laughing, trying to tackle each other into the water. Ben might have been slightly taller, but Pete had determination. He took a running leap at his lover, catching Ben in the stomach with his shoulder. They crashed into the shallow water, spluttering and coughing as they surfaced.

"Oh, you are in trouble, Mr. Montgomery," Ben warned. "You are in deep, deep trouble."

Pete grinned mischievously, daring Ben. Ben grinned back.

They splashed each other wildly, laughing and shouting in the bright sunshine, swimming away from shore. When they were chest-deep, Pete dove under the water, swimming close to Ben's legs, reaching out to grab them, making Ben shout.

Pete grabbed the bottom hem of Ben's swim trunks and pulled, earning another loud shout. Ben slapped at Pete's shoulders as he came up out of the water, spluttering and victorious. He raised one eyebrow, challenging, then calmly stepped out of his trunks, kicking them toward the surface so he could grab them in his hand.

"Just don't forget to hold on to them this time," Pete warned, before he ducked back under the water.

When they emerged from the water, after the shocking heat of mouths and bodies on ocean-chilled skin, and clambered, wobbly-legged and satiated, up the deserted beach, there was no one to notice they'd accidentally swapped swimsuits. Ben sat behind Pete on the chaise lounge, his legs wrapped around Pete's hips, gently toweling his hair; no one could keep the curls in Pete's hair like Ben. Pete leaned back. Ben wrapped his arms around Pete's shoulders, and they lay there and let the sun dry them the rest of the way.

It was a good dream.

He shifted on his bunk, trying to get comfortable. He missed Ben most when he'd woken up in the middle of the night, alone. He'd become so accustomed to having him in his bed—not in a sexual way, though that was undeniably wonderful, too. But just having the man he loved in his bed, laying next to him, warm and quietly breathing, soothed him in a way nothing else could. Nights like this, when he'd wake up in the middle of the night, unable to go back to sleep, he'd listen to Ben's breathing, the little lip smacks and murmurs Ben made as he dreamed. Sometimes he'd say little nonsense things and they'd have a conversation that would leave Pete aching with the effort not to laugh too hard and wake him. Pete would turn to him, shuffle his legs around, curl his knees behind Ben's, press his cold toes against Ben's warm feet and finally fall asleep with his nose pressed against Ben's shoulder. Hours later, he'd wake again, and find Ben perfectly fitted behind him, close and warm and perfect.

He twitched the thin blanket over his shoulder, pummeled the thin pillow into a better shape and tried to think about Ben.

* * *

TWO WEEKS LATER, BEN LEANED out of the bathroom where he'd been washing his face, as Gwen dropped her keys on the table near the hotel room door and threw herself on his bed.

Well, technically, *their* bed. Ben didn't really relish bunking with the boys in the band, and Gwen didn't really relish bunking alone. There was no way, shape or form in any sort of hell that they'd be "bunking," Ben had said with a meaningful glare. Gwen had pretended to pout, but given in graciously.

She had pointed out that the whispers and rumors now surrounding the tour could only help them. It would keep everyone from trying to figure out Ben's love life, and would give her a nice respite from the tabloids as well. Ben, so far as the papers could find out, was a well-dressed, handsome young man from the wholesome state of Indiana. Their relationship hadn't raised many eyebrows—clearly, Gwen was just looking for someone to push around and into her bed. Photographers followed them for about a week, but when all they caught was some boringly affectionate dinners and a stroll or two in a park, they'd given up.

Gwen was in the process of unhooking her garter belt, one foot propped up on the bed. Ben finished patting his face dry, already in his pajamas.

"Roll your stockings down, darling. They'll last longer," he said as he passed her on the way to his side of the bed.

"And how would you know, *darling*," Gwen shot back.

"I'm a tailor. I know fabrics, I know material. Silk doesn't like to be pulled on like that." He pulled the covers back neatly, slid into bed and lay down. He rolled to his side, curling himself around his pillow, sure to remain on His Side of the bed.

"Oh, it's not because you wear these sometimes?" Her eyebrow was raised, a mocking smile on her face.

"No. I don't wear stockings."

"Does your boy?"

"Peter. His name is Peter, might I remind you. And no, he doesn't either."

She was silent a moment, considering. He shot a dark look at her, but her face had changed. Instead of looking as though she was trying to offend, she looked honestly curious.

"Benny… how does it work?"

"How does what work?"

"You know. Relations. With a man. With two men." He was baffled. Gwen Andrews, the sex kitten? Gwen Andrews, the shocking seductress? Was she actually asking *him* about sex?

He looked at her severely, pushing himself up to lean against the headboard. "All right, Gwen Andrews. You open that bar over there, pour me a drink, and I'll explain a few things to you. But I am *not* having this conversation with you stone-cold sober."

"But... just... just tell me where he puts his—"

"Gwen! Booze, first. Salacious details, second."

* * *

"Okay, now tell me. Everything." Gwen sloshed her whiskey as she handed him a full glass and bounced to sit next to him on the bed.

Ben smiled wickedly. "Oh, I'm going to turn this all around on you, darling."

"On me?"

"Yes. Who was the last man you were in a relationship with?"

"Nicky. Nicky Gambino."

"And what did you love about him?"

"Oh, I love a man with broad shoulders. Nice and broad and strong shoulders. Gets me every time."

"Shoulders, yes. Shoulders are very nice. But what did you like about him, specifically? What drew you to him?"

"His shoulders."

"Christ, Gwen." Ben covered his eyes with one hand. "I mean, what sort of connection did you have, what about his brain or his heart attracted you?"

"He didn't have much going for him with his brain or his heart, actually. It was definitely his external organs that were attractin' me, if you catch my drift."

"After weeks on tour, sharing a hotel room with you, yes, I catch your drift." He sighed. He took another sip of his whisky and tried again. "Surely you must, at some point in your life, have been in love—like, really truly and deeply in love with someone."

Her eyes softened sadly. "Yes. Jack."

"What did you love about him?"

"He was sweet. And kind. And funny."

"And?"

"He was strong, and not just with his muscles, but he was—he was always a good person, no matter what."

"And?"

"He didn't bullshit me, and he always told me his honest opinion whether I was gonna like it or not."

"And what else?"

"What else?" She looked down at her glass, swirling the whiskey around. "He felt like home. Like I belonged to him. Like—like he and I belonged together. He just was home to me."

"And what was the first thing you noticed about him?"

"He had this light in his eyes. He was talking about starting a place, a club, to help kids stay out of trouble, and he was—he was lit up about it. He just glowed whenever he talked about helping kids. I couldn't keep my eyes off him. I just knew I had to talk to him some more."

"And do you ever dream about him?"

Her eyes flinched, a sharp hurt in them. She knocked back the rest of her whiskey in one gulp. "Yes."

"And what do you dream about him?"

She hesitated. "The feel of him next to me when I'd wake up in the middle of the night. Knowing that he was this huge giant man; he could bust up anything he wanted to, and when he'd get real angry, I could see all that strength just simmering inside him, but he never once even thought of using it to hurt me. That stinky man-smell when he'd been working hard and he'd come home all sweaty. I just loved the way he used to smell. The way he kissed me and I'd have whisker burn, and I'd pretend to complain about it, but it actually kind of turned me on."

"Oh, yes." Ben sighed. "Beard burn. Yes. That's always nice."

Gwen started out of her reverie and looked at him as though he was crazy.

"Pete's beard comes in fuller than mine. Usually, if he's not shaving, I'm not either. We're usually out at the beach for the weekend, or something. But his beard always seems to come in rougher, so I'm the one who winds up with beard burn." He finished his glass and poured them both another.

"And all you can do it just sit and wait until your face stops being so red—"

"Mmm-hmm," Ben agreed. "It usually goes away faster on my face than on my thighs, though."

"Your thighs?"

He widened his eyes meaningfully at her and couldn't help but laugh as he saw in her eyes the realizations fall into place, one by one, plinking like the last drops of milk into a bucket. The look of sheer gobsmacked amazement when she realized she knew exactly what he was just referring to made him guffaw with good-natured laughter.

She joined in, laughing and coughing and sputtering in her whiskey.

"It's not that different from you and Jack, what Pete and I have," Ben said, a pang in his heart at the thought of being so close to him—in the same country, but still so far away.

"All those things you loved about him," he continued, "those are all things I love about Pete. He's got that light that just draws me to him. He's got the greatest heart—no one has a bigger, kinder heart than Pete. He's ridiculously silly, and he's always making a fool of himself, trying to make me laugh—"

"You're really head over heels for him, aren't you?" Gwen asked quietly.

"I really am. And he's—you're exactly right. He's home to me. And I'm home to him. Whatever the world throws at us, we face it together. We're—he's everything to me. We're everything to each other."

"Oh, honey." Gwen sighed and dropped her head to his shoulder. "It's the same thing, isn't it?"

"Well, there may be a few minor points of difference." Ben rested his head on hers. He couldn't help teasing her. "I am not certain you appreciated your man's physique with the same exuberant fervor that I appreciate Pete's."

"Oh, the hell you say!" Gwen popped her head up and glared at him. Ben laughed.

"Once, when we stopped at the stop of the Ferris wheel in Atlantic City, he was just so gorgeous, I just couldn't wait—I gave Jack a—I... I used my hand to—you know—"

"Jerk him off?" Ben supplied, wryly.

"Oh my God!" Gwen giggled, clapping her hands over her mouth, then dropping them to bunch them in her nightgown. "Yes. Oh my God!"

"Yes, I'm familiar with this—"

"Oh my God!" she shrieked.

"I'm sorry to disturb your delicate sensibilities," he said wryly, looking down at his glass of whiskey, empty once again, then closed one eye to try to see how much whiskey was left in the bottle, "but I've had a bit more to drink than I thought."

"Now you need to tell me!"

"Tell you what?"

"Your craziest, you know." She waggled her hands suggestively.

Ben had the fleeting thought that maybe he shouldn't. It was really none of her business, it was no one's business but his and Pete's. But, even talking about him a little bit, sharing even just a fragment of Pete had eased the ache in his chest he'd been living with every day since he last saw him. He knew the ache, the loneliness, the wistful yearning wouldn't go away, not until they were together again. And he hoped, if he talked with Gwen about him, maybe for a little bit, he could bring Pete to life, here, and be with him. He hoped just to be whole again, for a little while.

He told her of an impromptu romantic picnic, long ago and late at night, in deserted Gramercy Park, the private park to which only they and their neighbors had keys. How they'd winced as they'd unlocked the gates, which squeaked open on the nearly silent street. How the full moon cast shadows over the gracious lawns and dignified flowerbeds. How they'd spread a blanket under a stand of trees then shared cake and a bottle of wine, listening to the birds settling down in the hot summer night. How they'd kept silent themselves, lips drawn to bodies like magnets, tasting and cherishing, the leaves of the trees dappling shadows on their skin in the moonlight. How Pete had tasted of salt and musk and something earthy and warm. How Ben had muffled his own moans with the edge of the blanket when it was his turn. How they'd dressed with trembling limbs and whispering laughter, then gathered their things and stumbled home to sleep the rest of the night in each other's arms.

"Oh, honey." Gwen sighs. "He sounds like such a sweetheart."

"He *is* a sweetheart. Just ask my sister."

"Your sister *knows?*" Gwen looked scandalized.

"I introduced him to her a month after we met. They adore each other. When we go to Indiana, we stay with her in Indianapolis. My father is—It's complicated with my dad."

"Does he know?"

"All he'll admit to is that my roommate is a hell of a nice guy I've known for quite a few years now. We don't discuss it any further than that. Ever."

"And Pete's parents?"

"They act as if I'm an old friend of Pete's. They even pretend to try to set me up with various cousins and friends of the family whenever we visit them."

Gwen snorted, indelicately. "Oh, I bet that goes over well."

Ben leaned his head back against the wall, running his tongue over his upper lip. "I don't really need to… explain about him and me to anyone. We know, and that's what's important. Though, his mother's been warming up to me."

"Oh, since Pete's disappearance?"

A vast hole seemed to appear in front of Ben. There was no air around him, but he didn't care; he had to remind himself to take another breath. *He's okay, Ben. He's okay. He's been found. You got those letters from him. Ginger saw him with her own two eyes. He's okay.*

"Wow, honey, it still really upsets you." Gwen was eyeing him with bleary concern. "You're shaking. Honey, it's okay. He's okay."

"Right. He's okay. For now." Ben smiled bleakly. "At least, last I heard."

"But, no news is good news, right?" she whispered.

"Most of the time, yes. His brother has our tour itinerary, and promised to telephone or send a telegram if he heard anything…"

"C'mere, honey. Snuggle with me before it's time for lights out."

"It was time for lights out *hours* ago, Gwennie."

She switched off the light on the bedside table, and turned to him, cooing. "How you want your snuggles tonight, Benny?"

"Oh God, again, Gwen?"

"I sleep better cuddled up. And you know you want me well rested."

"Oh hell yes, I do." Honestly, Ben really didn't mind—it was actually kind of comforting. It was nice to have a warm body—a friend, when he couldn't have his lover—to sleep next to. His nightmares weren't so frequent or so violent with Gwen there.

"No, no, no, you're sleeping on my chest tonight, Gwennie. Waking up with your boobs under my face is terrifying to me."

"But they're such nice boobs." Gwen pouted, peering down at them.

"Yes, dear. They are lovely." He held out his arms, and she curled her body into his. "Just like you."

"Aww, gee, Benny. You're swell." She reached up to pet his cheek.

"Thanks, honey. No matter what I say while I'm sober, I think you're swell too."

She yawned widely. "G'night, Benny."

"G'night, sweetie."

They were both asleep within minutes.

* * *

AFTER THE LONG, ARDUOUS TRIP to their first concert overseas, Gwen, Ben and the rest of their entourage were exhausted. It was cold and foggy and dismal when they landed in England only to find that a key trunk of costumes had gone missing somehow. All of Gwen's gowns—as well as some of the costumes for the rest of the girls—were sitting on the tarmac in New York.

Gwen started screaming, throwing things, pitching fits. She fired everyone in sight; no one budged. They were all fired at least once a week.

Ben sidled over to a corporal, who was standing open-mouthed in the doorway. A few whispered requests met with an emphatic agreement from the soldier, and Ben was soon in possession of several pieces of material. He slipped out, feeling Gwen's wrath shaking the walls, grabbed his sewing kit from his suitcase, found a quiet corner and began to sew.

A few moments later, he presented a still-raging Gwen with a small stack of cloth.

"What's this?" she snarled.

"Your costume. You're going to freeze your keister off, but the show starts in twenty minutes, so I suggest you put that on so we can do the final fitting."

"Benny? What the hell—"

"Gwen," he said sternly. "Put. It. On."

The other men were hurriedly ushered out. Gwen slipped on the costume. The corporal had raided the supply room and brought him an officer's shirt, the smallest he could find, and two bright red signal flags. Ben had tailored the shirt to Gwen's bust size and sewn the flags together to make a very short skirt. It barely needed adjustments. Gwen was amazed: it was patriotic, yet sexy. The soldiers were sure to love it.

Some bright red shoes, a pilfered officer's cap, some lipstick and she was ready.

The rest of the girls were having trouble—their costumes had arrived but were damp.

Jeanette, a dark haired girl with wintry gray eyes, wanted to wear her coat while performing.

"I'm gonna die of cold wearing that thing," she whined, pointing at her red dress drying on its hanger.

"Ben?" Gwen asked.

"No, there's no way. I can't make any more; we have to go on in less than ten minutes!"

"Then, Jeanette, you're gonna have to put it on." Gwen's voice was steely.

"What if I say no?"

"Jeanette, you put on the fucking dress. All of you!" Gwen wheeled to address everyone in the room, spitting through her teeth. "Put on your fucking dresses. And you powder your nose and you put on your fucking heels and your fucking lipstick and you fucking smile. I don't care how cold you are. I don't care how miserable you are. You think that's anything compared to what these boys have gone through?"

There was silence in the room as the girls all stared at Gwen. They'd seen her wildly throwing things, screaming and carrying on. This new, quiet vehemence, growled expletives and orders being spat through clenched teeth, this was new and no one seemed to know what to make of it.

"You put on your brightest lipstick, you drown yourself in your most feminine cologne and you smile. These boys are going to get the best show we can give them, and that show starts from the minute you walk out this door. You pick the part you want to play and you stick to it until we are back on that plane. You be the vamp, the vixen, the whore or the golly-gee fucking girl next door. I don't care. These boys have gone through—are *still* going through hell—and we are here to remind them what they're fighting for."

She continued, "And I don't really give a fuck what you think. All I know is that it's *my name* on that plane out there, and if you give those boys anything less than *every fucking ounce of everything* you have, then you are fucking going to have to figure out how you're gonna swim home. You got it?"

Gwen stormed out to her private dressing room to reapply her crimson lipstick. Ben was the only one to see the tears welling in her eyes.

* * *

THREE SHOWS, THREE HOSPITAL TOURS. Gwen really was giving it her all, and the rest of crew had stepped up to the challenge. The shows were no difficult matter, but after every hospital round, Gwen would lock herself and Ben into her private dressing room and sob in his arms.

"They all look like Jack," she wailed. Jack, she finally sobbed, had been her sweetheart since high school. Their relationship was kept secret by the public relations department of her movie studio. He'd enlisted, been wounded in action, and sent home. He'd committed suicide after his arm had had to be amputated.

"He didn't think I would love a man with only one arm. I don't know why. He didn't even give me a chance to show him—" she could barely whisper into Ben's arms.

"So that's why you're so always over the top with them—the soldiers."

"I need to show them that there's someone who cares. That it doesn't matter how many arms or legs they have, someone finds them attractive and lovable; I just need them to know that someone cares."

She wept after every hospital tour, but by the time it was concert-time, it never showed. She was energetic, vivacious, flirtatious and outrageous. She requested the names of soldiers in advance, so she could pull them up on stage and sing to them—curling herself in their laps, twining herself around them, much to the jealously howling delight of their compatriots.

Just before the fourth show, Gwen announced a set change. The girls would close the show while Ben and Rodney, the very, very dull bass they'd found in Kansas City, would sit out the last six songs. Ben's voice was feeling the chill. He'd been babying it with hot tea. *God, no one makes tea like the English,* he thought.

They'd cut one of his solos; tonight, he was just singing "The Very Thought of You." As always, he closed his eyes against the blinding stage lights and thought of Pete while he sang it.

Immediately after he'd left the stage, Vicki rushed up to him. "Gwen says she's popped a seam. Can you fix it?"

"My kit's in the dressing room." He eyed Gwen, onstage, joking with the crowd. He couldn't see anything wrong with her seams. "I'll run back and get it."

He fumbled his way through the makeshift backstage to the small office that had been provided for Gwen's private dressing area. He rushed in and fumbled over the desk, trying to find his kit in the inevitable piles of stockings and scarves and just *things* she seemed to leave behind.

Ah, there it was. He unrolled it to be sure he had enough of the right thread. And found a note.

Oops. I was wrong, the seams are fine. Wait here. Xoxo Gwennie.

As he stood there, looking confused at the note, he heard a knock on the door.

"Excuse me? Miss Andrews?" Through the door, the voice was muffled.

"She's onstage." Ben was still trying to figure out what the hell she meant; she was obviously plotting something, and that always made Ben a little nervous. He sneezed, wiping his nose on his handkerchief.

"Gesundheit, Benjamin. Now are you going to let me in, or do I have to stand out here in the hall all night?" said the voice on the other side of the door.

Ben ran for the door. He couldn't believe it'd taken him so long to recognize that voice.

CHAPTER TEN

"Did you know that Ben is also singing with the USO?" Pete said as he shuffled down the row of chairs set up in one of the hangars. Other soldiers were milling around, finding seats and chatting loudly before the show began.

"No, really?" Ginger dropped heavily into the folding chair next to him, rocking affectionately into his shoulder.

"I just got a letter from him a few days ago." Pete stretched his long legs out against the chairs in front of him. "He was filling in at the canteen for a singer who was late. He did almost a whole set, and when she arrived, she signed him on the spot. Amazing, hunh?"

"Amazing," Ginger murmured, watching the crowd filing into the seats around them.

"Guess who he's singing with?" Pete whispered.

Ginger just grinned, one eyebrow raised.

"Gwen Andrews." Pete grinned back. "Can you believe it? *The* Gwen Andrews heard Ben singing and recognized his talent, and I'm just so proud my buttons are about to pop off."

"Off your pants or off your jacket?" Ginger waggled her eyebrows at him.

"Oh stop, you."

She slapped at his arm. "You stop."

"No, you." Pete grabbed her hand and trapped it in the crook of his arm, both out of affection and knowing she wouldn't be able to use it again in retaliation.

A loud drumroll grabbed everyone's attention. A young private shuffled awkwardly to the microphone and squinted into the spotlight.

"Ladies and gentleman, would you please take your seats?" His voice cracked on the last word, and he cleared his throat roughly. "The Gwen Andrews Singers are about ready to take the stage—"

"Did he just say Gwen Andrews?" Pete grabbed Ginger's arm in a vise grip.

Ginger just nodded, beaming at him.

"Are you serious?" Pete shrieked.

Ginger clapped her hand over his mouth, smiling apologetically at the soldiers in front of them, who'd turned around to peer curiously at them both.

"Sorry. He's just really excited about finally seeing Gwen Andrews." She smiled genially. "He's just a really, really big fan of hers, you know?"

Pete's eyes were dancing over Ginger's hand, still tightly over his mouth.

"Yes, you idiot." She laughed at him, then whispered, "He's here, but he needs to do the show first."

"He's really here? And he's—he's all right and he's fine and he's here?"

"Stop babbling like a fool. Yes, he's here. He'll be onstage in just a few minutes."

"Oh my God, Red." Pete sat back in his chair, dumbfounded. "Oh dear God."

"Gwen's got a whole plan, all set to surprise you both. He doesn't know you're here, either. She's been working with Corporal Johnson over there, to coordinate getting you here," she hissed as the lights abruptly dimmed.

"Without further ado," a voice boomed over the speakers, "the USO is proud to present The Gwen Andrews Singers!"

"Whoa there, cowboy," Ginger whispered as she leaned against Pete's shoulder. He grabbed her hand tightly. "We all know what's going to happen if you rush up there on that stage. Just keep your cute little ass in your chair, and we'll sneak you backstage before the show's over so you can be with him. Just hold your horses."

"Oh my God, Red," Pete's eyes were shining in the reflected light as he watched the stage eagerly. "Oh my God."

PETE STOOD IN THE DIM hallway, the music loud behind him, and waited for Ben to open the door. It seemed he could tell the moment Ben recognized his voice and came sprinting for the door. The door barely escaped being wrenched from its hinges, and there was Ben—*Benjamin, oh God Ben, you're even more beautiful than I remember*—face flushed, smiling broadly, ready to launch himself into Pete's arms.

Pete retained enough presence of mind to reach out with his hands—hands that wanted to cup Ben's face gently, run through his glorious hair, snake around his waist, grab fiercely at his hips, skate across every plane and shape and surface of Ben's skin—to curl around Ben's shoulders and push him back into the room, then slam the door shut behind them. Then their lips crashed together and Pete could feel nothing but Benjamin. *Ben, oh God Ben, you're here; you're really here, and this is so much better than my dreams.*

Ben barely had time to register the hair—*oh God, that hair*—and the bright melting-honey eyes of Pete—*Peter, Pete, Peter, oh God, he's here.*

There were so many things Ben wanted to say: *I love you, oh God, I love you; how are you here; how did you know I was here; what are you doing here; God. kiss me again; I love you so much; don't cry, Benjamin, don't cry* but his mouth was busy on Pete's—devouring him and being devoured in turn.

There was no finesse to it—they were far too needy for subtlety. Their teeth clacked together; their lips were soon sore and swollen. Ben realized Pete had his shirt already half untucked from his trousers and was scrabbling at the skin of his waist.

"We've got three more songs until Gwen Andrews and the rest of the world comes barreling through that door like a barn on fire."

"Twelve minutes, then." Pete kicked off his shoes, hurriedly unbuckled his belt and dropped his uniform on the floor, still kissing Ben frantically.

"Plus the curtain calls. And maybe an encore." Ben managed to bend down—still kissing Pete, who followed him awkwardly to the floor, unwilling to stop kissing him—to grab Pete's uniform. He swiftly draped it over a chair, "We're going—*kiss, kiss*—to have enough questions—*kiss, kiss, kiss*—without having to explain—*kiss, kiiiiiiiiiiisss*—why the hell your uniform looks like it's been run over by a tank."

Pete stopped kissing him. Ben turned his attention from the uniform to Pete's face. He was flushed; his eyes were wide and staring. Pete reached his fingertips up to brush along Ben's face, gently tracing his cheekbones down to his jaw.

"I… I know, baby. I know. But, we've got twelve minutes when we know we're alone…" Ben slipped off his trousers off as Pete sucked in a trembling breath. They wrapped their arms around each other, crashing their lips together again. Pete dragged his lips down Ben's neck, spreading his shirt collar wide to suck at his collarbone.

Pete let out a ragged breath. "Ben?" His voice was so needy, so small and broken.

"I'm here, baby. I'm here. We're here, together."

Pete put both hands on Ben's face to kiss him. "Please. I need you," he whispered.

He lifted Ben up to sit on the desk. Ben leaned himself back against the wall, curling his back and scooting his hips forward.

Pete spit into his hand; it wasn't ideal, but it's what they had. He leaned forward to kiss Ben—*oh God, Ben, Ben, Ben, oh God.*

It was rough, too little glide and too much burn and definitely not romantic, this time. Too much need, too many months apart, too much time, too much to reclaim and relearn; and it didn't matter—it was the fastest way back to each other. It was them, the two of them, and neither one of them could bear the thought of being any farther apart any longer.

There was a knock on the door.

"Benny? It's Ginger. And Gwen. The show's over."

Pete was cleaned up and dressed in seconds. "Well, you can't fly a bomber in your pajamas," he whispered, grinning. "The weather's so rotten here, we have to be ready to go on a moment's notice once the clouds break. Sometimes, we don't get much warning."

"Just a moment!" Ben said brightly, then wiped his stomach frantically with his handkerchief, rearranged his clothes and swiped a hand through his hair. He nodded and Pete opened the door.

Ginger pushed past Pete to launch herself at Ben with a squealed "Hi, honey!" Pete extended his hand to take the large basket Gwen held awkwardly and grinned at her.

"So, this is him?" Gwen gave Pete a critical once-over as she pulled the door shut behind her.

"This is him." Ben couldn't help but grin as he caught Pete's eye.

"Oh, watch out, Gwennie." Ginger sighed, the two of them fast friends already. "These two are so in love, they'll make you puke."

"So in love, eh?" Gwen was still eyeing Pete.

"We sure are." Pete sighed, holding out his hand to Ben. His shy smile changed to a bright beam when Ben took his hand and held it tightly.

"Yes, I can see that," Gwen said drily. Her nostrils flared, taking in the unmistakable bleachy scent. "I can smell it too."

Pete choked back an embarrassed laugh. Ben glared at her.

"What? Oh, Benny, don't be such a prude." Gwen stuck out her tongue at Ben, who reciprocated. Pete felt an easing in his chest at the sight—Ben hadn't been alone all this time. He's had someone to spar with.

"Now, it's lovely to meet you and all, Pete. May I call you Pete?" Gwen smiled winningly at him as he nodded. "But, I'm sure you have better things to do with your time than chit-chat with me all night. So, let go of your boy and give me a boost, will you?"

"A boost?"

"Well, obviously, Ginger and I will not be staying here for dinner this evening. She and I have already made plans. Benny, here," she said, smirking at him, "has a lot of—frustrations he needs to get out of his system. He's frequently so frustrated that he's mouthy and argumentative and just a general pain in the ass. So, I expect you to return him to me satiated and utterly exhausted and docile and compliant."

At Ben's snort of amusement, she smirked. "Fine. I'll settle for utterly exhausted."

Gwen continued, motioning toward the basket. "I personally sweet-talked a lot of people to get us a romantic dinner for four. Any nosy nellies will think the four of us are in here all night long, and whatever conclusions they come to had better be far less scandalous than what actually happens in here—or Peter, I'm gonna know that Benjamin's been exaggerating your skills in bed."

Pete wasn't quite sure what to say to that, so he settled for giving Gwen a cheeky kiss and a knowing wink. She slapped him on the ass, saying, "I do believe you'll do, Montgomery. You'll do."

Ginger clambered up on the desk to poke her head out the window. "The crates we stacked are still there. You grab that bottle while I kiss Benny and we'll be out of your hair, Pete. Don't forget, we've got to be back at base by nine a.m."

She jumped back down off the desk as Gwen rifled through the basket, pulling out two bottles of wine and setting one back on the desk before shoving the other inside her coat. Ginger gave Ben a loud smacking kiss on the lips. He hugged her tightly.

"Take care of yourself, Red, you hear me?" he whispered. "I don't know how you managed this, but thank you."

"It was all Gwen. I just provided the excuse to get Prince Charming over here. The entire base is already convinced we're fucking—it's a good cover for both of us," she said earnestly, then screwed up her nose. "Though I might have to provide a pregnancy scare soon, just to keep it in interesting."

Ben chuckled, still holding her. "Thank you, sweetheart."

Pete put his hand on Ginger's hair, caressing gently. "Honestly, Red. Thank you. I'll pick you up at the tea shop in the morning, so we can ride back to base together?"

Ginger eyed Gwen, now climbing up on the desk, appraisingly. "I don't know where the hell she got a hold of that wine and I'm not exactly sure what she's got planned for the rest of the night, but I have the feeling it's going to be exhausting. But, yes, I'll be at the tea shop, whenever you get there."

"Now, boys, don't forget to lock the door." Gwen turned and smiled graciously at them. "I've put the fear of God into everyone I can think of—tantrums of epic proportions and my wrath will rain down upon anyone who dares disturb 'us' tonight. But, don't be stupid."

Ben crossed to the door quickly, snapping the lock shut as Pete reached up to help boost Gwen out the window. She wriggled a bit, her ankles

flailing, then dropped out of sight. A muffled thump and a faint "fuck"—
and she was gone. Ginger gave Ben a last quick kiss, winked at Pete and
scrambled out the window and into the night.

Pete shook out the blanket that covered the basket and spread it on
the floor. He knelt and began unpacking the food.

Suddenly, he felt awkward, unsure how to act. He knew how to be
Captain Peter Montgomery. He thought he remembered how to be just
regular Peter Montgomery. He just couldn't figure out how to be both at
the same time.

Captain Montgomery would not have just fucked someone without
pleasantries or seduction or, hell, even really saying "hello." Captain
Montgomery had duties and dignity and rules and regulations to uphold
and follow.

Captain Montgomery would not be staring lewdly at his lover's neck—
his lover who was now stretched out full-length on the blanket next to
him, his legs long and limber, leaning back against his elbow. Captain
Montgomery's cock would not be already throbbing again at the sight of
Ben's fingers deftly re-loosening his tie, exposing his neck—that luscious
neck where Pete knows just the spot to nibble to make Ben moan. Captain
Montgomery was now entirely distracted and had been kneeling in one
spot, with a packet of crackers suspended in the air for some time now.
He dropped them and folded himself more comfortably on the blanket.

Ben had picked up an apple, taken out his pocketknife and was busy
peeling it. Pete didn't know why—they both like eating the apple with the
peel. Now he was busy fussing with the peels, fussing with the blanket.

It struck him—Ben was nervous too.

"This is… odd. I feel odd. Do you feel odd?" Pete stammered, earning
a relieved smile and nod from Ben.

He reached to take the knife from Ben's hand and set it on the shelf,
then stretched himself out next to him, moving the picnic basket out of
the way. He pushed on his shoulders until Ben was laying on his back,
then lay carefully next to him, resting his head on Ben's chest.

"We'll just stay like this until we're used to each other again." Pete
hoped he sounded light-hearted.

"I'll never get used to you," Ben tried to tease back, but his voice broke.

They both were quiet, Ben running his hands through Pete's hair, Pete just trying to keep the tears held back as he listened to Ben's heart beating under his ear.

Pete realized he'd be completely and perfectly happy if this were the only thing he could hear for the rest of his life—just Ben's heart, strong and vital; if the only things he could feel for the rest of his life were Ben's chest rising and falling steadily beneath his cheek and Ben's breath gently rustling the curls on his forehead. His patriotic zeal had dimmed a bit since coming over here; there was so much pointless death and destruction on every side. And while he was determined that right and good will eventually prevail, really all he was fighting for was the right to go back home, to this man—to Ben, *his* Ben—and live the rest of their lives together in peace and harmony. He clutched his fingers in Ben's shirt, daring anyone to take him away.

Suddenly, Pete's stomach growled, breaking the tension and making them both laugh.

Pete shifted to sit up, but Ben pulled him back down, shaking his head. "Too far away," he whispered.

Pete understood.

They awkwardly shifted to pull the picnic basket toward them with their feet—snaking their ankles around the basket and laughing like children. Somehow they got the basket close enough to reach inside and pull out their dinner—a vegetable stew flavored with beef, several slices of brown bread and a small bottle of apple juice. They fed each other awkwardly, still curled together, laughing when the food got in Pete's nose instead of his mouth, when the crumbs fell down Ben's shirt, tickling him. They grabbed the wine from the shelf and shared one wineglass, lovingly holding it between them.

Much later, after feeding turned into sucking fingers and droplets of wine needed to be licked off lips, after clothes were removed slowly and skin was kissed reverently, when they were holding each other, blinking sleepily and happily at each other, Pete softly nuzzled his nose against Ben's and thought, *Now I can die a happy man.*

THE BRIGHTENING SKY OUTSIDE THE small windows set high in the wall woke Ben first. They were lying on their sides, facing each other, wrapped in the rough Army blanket. Pete was drooling on Ben's bicep and snoring loudly. Ben's arm had gone entirely numb with the weight of Pete's head. One of his nostrils was crusted with snot, thanks to his cold and runny nose.

It was a decidedly unromantic, prosaic and mundane way to wake—and Ben wished it would never end. He disentangled himself as gently as he could, propping himself up awkwardly to wipe his nose.

Pete stirred and wiped at his face.

"Good morning, beautiful," Ben whispered.

"Good morning, gorgeous." Pete's voice was rough and low. He flipped his wrist over to read the glowing numbers on his watch.

"Mmm, another hour before I have to meet Red." Pete cleared his throat and rolled to his back, blinking sleepily. "Come back here and snuggle with me."

"I need a handkerchief, first. My nose is going to run off my face."

"I've got an extra one in my pants pocket," Pete murmured. "If we know where those went."

Ben laughed. "They're—somewhere. I think they're over there by the hat stand?"

"Well, wipe it on the napkin and come back here quick. I haven't had enough of being close to you yet."

Ben found not one but two napkins crumpled in the basket. He put them within reach, then stretched out again next to Pete, laying his head on Pete's chest.

"How did you know I was here?" he asked, softly.

"I didn't," Pete chuckled. "Ginger did. Somehow, she'd been plotting with our company clerk, who'd been plotting with Gwen. She and I had liberty—we weren't on duty. She said she had to deliver some supplies here and wanted some company for the ride. This isn't actually our base. She and I are stationed about ten miles away."

He settled Ben's head more comfortably on his shoulder, and continued. "And even though she looked like a cat that swallowed a canary, even when we were heading into the hanger to find a seat, I didn't have any idea. I thought there was a movie showing, until the band came out."

"And then you knew?"

"I hoped. I only got your letter saying you were coming overseas last week. I didn't dare hope you'd be coming here, now." Pete's arms tightened around Ben. "When you came out on stage, B, she nearly had to sit on my lap to keep me from running up there and throwing myself on you."

Ben chuckled. "That would have been difficult to explain."

"And then you started singing and I thought I'd died and gone to heaven. Really, Benny. You're incredible."

"Thank you." Ben pressed a kiss to Pete's shoulder.

"And somehow, Ginger and Gwen have been in cahoots. I don't know how it happened—and I don't think I want to know how, really. The two of them together—" he said, shaking his head, "they're a frightening force of nature."

"Oh God, yes," Ben agreed.

"And when you left the stage, Ginger told me where to find you. And I flat-out sprinted to get back here, and you started sneezing and I almost broke down the door."

"And now, here we are." Ben smiled.

"Here we are. And we've got—" he said, checking his watch, "exactly fifty-two minutes until I have to leave, so c'mere, you."

Ben grinned, rolling over on top of him, and the rest of their time passed far too quickly.

* * *

THE NEXT DAY, THE TOUR moved to Pete's base. Ben sat in the office designated as Gwen's private dressing room, mending costumes. The girls' high heels were murder on the hems of their gowns; one of them kept popping her zipper and sequins were dropping like flies. Gwen sauntered in, dropped her coat, hat and gloves on the table, then checked her lipstick, which was smudged from kissing the gauntlet of soldiers waiting for her. She was flushed and giggling—one (or more) of them must have been cute.

Sharp footsteps sounded down the hall, and then Pete was there, dress uniform sharply pressed, officer's cap tucked snugly under his arm. The belt around the jacket accentuated his slim waist, the insignia on the boards at his shoulders emphasized their breadth. His hair was styled just so; his shoes were bright with polish. He was so beautiful, Ben felt he couldn't breathe.

Gwen invited him in and shut the door behind him. Pete snapped his heels together as he nodded thanks. Ben recognized the look in Pete's eyes, afraid if either of them blinked, this would all be a dream, and neither of them would really be here.

Pete rushed to Ben, dropping his cap on the table in front of him, swooping down to capture Ben's mouth as he sat in his chair. Ben kissed him back, feverishly and without self-consciousness—he really couldn't care less that Gwen was standing there. Their day apart—Pete to his duty roster, Ben to his show preparations—had been too long.

"Boys," she whispered. "I'm just going to pop out of here now. Ben, don't forget that the show's at four. And for Christ's sake, lock the door behind me."

Pete broke away, blushing and attempting to brush his disheveled hair back into place with his hands. "Uhhh. Sorry. Sorry. I just…"

"It's okay, honey. I can only imagine what it's like to have him here," she said, smiling wistfully.

"No, ummm, the boys would like to meet you. Both. I mean, they don't know about… they know I have a relative on your tour, and they'd really like to meet *my cousin, Ben*. And, of course, they're wild about you, Gwen. I'm supposed to bring you out to see the plane, and meet the rest of the crew."

Ben folded his work, putting everything in order. He combed his fingers through his hair, smoothing his trousers as he stood. Pete couldn't help but rake his eyes over his lover's lean body. Gwen cleared her throat, patting her hair into place.

"Benny, hand me my lipstick. And spritz me some more perfume. If I disappoint Pete's crew, I'll never be able to live with myself."

A FEW MINUTES LATER, THEY strode carefully down the flight line towards Pete's plane. Pete, with his cap now jauntily on his head, tucked Gwen's hand under his arm. Ben walked on her other side—any closer to Pete and he wouldn't be responsible for his actions.

As they got closer to the plane, Ben could see the crew ranged out around it, cleaning and inspecting. He hadn't realized how large B-17 bombers were, as Pete pointed out the different parts of it. A huge glass cone served as the nose of the plane, where the bombardier would sit to target their bombs. A bubble of glass about a third of the way back on the top, just behind the cockpit, was the top gun turret. Ben had to duck to see the ball turret hanging under the plane's belly about halfway back. Each turret could spin, to provide better gun coverage. The large doors three quarters of the way back were open; the waist gunner's guns loomed out. He could just see the tail gun's pair of muzzles.

When the crew saw Gwen, they all jumped to their feet, brushing dirt and grass from their uniforms. Everyone lined up to be introduced to Pete's friends—barely paying any attention to Ben, eyes only for Gwen.

The crew clambered up in the plane, hoisting Gwen up—each eager to show her his place and responsibility. They promptly forgot Ben and Pete, still standing outside.

Pete walked Ben to the front, toward the huge glass nose cone, and pointed up. Just under the front cockpit windows, painted on the side of the plane was a long-legged woman, dressed in dungarees and a work shirt. She smiled coyly over her shoulder as she held a rivet gun, golden-red hair peeped out of a handkerchief tied around her head. "Riveting Redhead" was written underneath in swirling yellow letters.

Ben raised his eyebrow. "You picked this out?"

"I couldn't name her 'Ben,' now, could I?"

"Her?"

"Planes are always 'her.' Just like ships."

"And my hair is not red."

"Is, too." Pete couldn't help but tease.

"Is not." Ben stared up at the plane, and Pete could see the stubborn jut of his jaw. Ben had always been particularly strident about *not* being a redhead.

So Pete leaned close, murmuring in Ben's ear. "Well, I wasn't actually referring to the hair you show in public."

Ben pretended to glare at him, then softened. "And you named her after me?"

"Yes. Well, I won the coin toss—and the boys liked my idea anyway, so everyone was happy."

Ben smiled at him. Pete grinned widely.

"But, look closer. I gave very specific instructions."

Ben stepped closer and craned his neck to look at the painting. First he noticed the eyes. Bright blue, cat-shaped, with long brown lashes. His eyes. Those were almost his cheekbones, and something of his mouth, as well—almost too wide, with full lips. It was definitely his smile.

"Come on," Pete said softly. "Come see my spot."

Ben watched as Pete easily hoisted himself into the belly of the plane, eyes sparkling. Ben was less graceful, but managed. No one was watching him anyway.

"Careful here. Watch your head."

They scrambled up to the cockpit, two chairs side-by-side with a small space between them. Pete motioned for Ben to sit in the left side, the captain's chair, and sat in the co-pilot's seat. The cockpit smelled of leather seats, hot metal baking in the sun and the pungent tang of engine oil. Ben delicately ran his fingertips over the controls, his hands over the stick.

Stuck in the bezel around one gauge was a small snapshot—Ben recognized it easily. He and Bets and Pete—their arms slung around each other, sitting on a couch at a party. Pete was kissing Bets on the cheek. Bets' head was thrown back; her mouth was wide open, obviously cackling. Ben was looking straight at the camera, his eyes bright with laughter.

"It's the first thing on my pre-flight checklist. I put it in in my flight jacket pocket, and every time we land, it comes back out and goes right here. It's my good luck charm." Pete said softly. "I told them it's the best picture I have of my sweetheart back home. It's the only one I carry of you. It's what reminds me that I need to come home, every time."

Ben's lips trembled. He wished he could reach out his hand, wished Pete would take it. But the crew was just beginning to clamber out of the plane, making all sorts of ridiculous comments and succeeding in making Gwen laugh loudly.

"Every song I sing… it's for you," Ben whispered. "It's always been for you."

The charged moment passed, then Charlie poked his head in, "Cap'n, this lady says she's parched and needs a drink."

"And we all know you can't keep a lady waiting!" Pete grinned rakishly at Ben, and they scrambled out of the plane.

* * *

CHARLIE COULDN'T HELP BUT NOTICE the quiet glow from Pete as they walked along the flight line toward the officer's club. He just— he looked so happy. Like he couldn't hold it in, like he couldn't contain it. He walked with his head down, looking mostly at his feet and smiling at his spit-shined boots with a grin that just kept breaking through.

At first, he thought it was being around Gwen Andrews. She was flirtatious and gorgeous and famous and funny and he had a hard time not making an ass of himself around her. But then, no. That wasn't quite it, either.

He caught one glance Pete darted toward Ben, and it all fell into place: Pete being kind of cagey about his "sweetheart" back home, not really joining in when all the other guys got riled up about Betty Grable's legs, not having a pin-up girl in his locker.

Charlie knew sometimes he wasn't always the sharpest tack in the box, but he knew real love when he saw it.

THAT NIGHT, THE CONCERT WAS amazing. Inside one of the vast hangars, emptied of planes for the show, balloons and crepe paper streamers were hung. The crowd loved the banter between Gwen and Ben. They cheered raucously when Gwen announced, "at random," the name of Captain Montgomery. They pushed him up on stage, catcalling and whistling, for Gwen to sing, "I've Got a Crush on You" while perched in his lap. Pete, never one to back down from a challenge, played along, holding her hips securely and waggling his eyebrows at the crowd, earning more cheers and hollers from his comrades.

Ben stood to the side, loving every minute of it. This time, knowing Pete was sitting right there, so close he could almost touch him, he didn't need to close his eyes when it was time for him to sing. He found Pete's face back in the crowd, Pete's eyes glowing in the dim light, and sang just to him. For him.

Gwen's Private Picnic Basket was again waiting in her dressing room, along with a just-arrived Ginger, when the concert ended. Ben raised his eyebrow, as Pete plucked it up, along with the blanket, hung it over his forearm and ushered them all outside.

Night was just beginning to fall. Gwen and Ginger discreetly peeled themselves away as they passed the last barracks. Ben hadn't been able to get out of Gwen what the two of them had been up to, but he had his suspicions.

Pete led the way off-base, into the countryside. After a short walk, they found a dense stand of trees.

"Privacy," Pete whispered. He spread out the blanket in a small clearing, with a beautiful view of the ocean beyond.

They ate slowly, simple sandwiches with cheese, savoring the food and their time together, talking quietly. The summer night was warm, and they tangled themselves around each other, safe from prying eyes. They talked of everything, and nothing—mundane daily life and hopeful dreams. They mock-argued over new drapes for the dining room, what time of year they'd finally go to Miami, planning their lives once they were at home together again.

Sometime after the sun set and dark really fell, they both fell asleep, Pete curled around Ben's back, their hands intertwined.

PETE WOKE TO A SHARP kick to his shins, an elbow to his ribs. Benjamin. He was struggling in his sleep, struggling to get away. His breath was coming in short pants, his face contorted, tears sliding down his face from behind his closed eyelids.

"Benjamin," he whispered. "Benny, you're having a nightmare. It's okay." Ben continued to struggle, writhing in the blankets.

"Ben," Pete said firmly, "you need to wake up. It's just a dream, baby." He shook his shoulder slightly, then more strongly.

Ben's eyes opened, frantically searching. He reached out with both hands, grabbing at Pete's shoulders.

"It's me, baby," Pete comforted. "It's just me."

Ben shuddered, running his hands down Pete's arm, clenching Pete's hands. "Oh God. I…" He shook his head, tears still streaming.

"Baby, you're okay. Everything's okay, B. It's just me."

"I dreamed you were hurt. You were hurt, and I couldn't find you."

"I was hurt, baby, but not anymore. I'm okay. It's okay."

"You were screaming," Ben sobbed. "You were screaming and begging me… and I did everything I could, but I couldn't find you."

"Shh." Pete clutched Ben to his chest. "It's okay, baby. I'm here. I was hurt, but I'm fine now. I was lost, but they found me."

"I just… I just couldn't… and oh God, Pete, I couldn't find you." Ben's sobs rocked them both.

"Hey now. Hey, love. It's okay. It's okay now. I'm okay. It's okay."

"There's always fog. And mist. And I can hear you, but I can't ever see you. And you're begging… you're hurt and you're begging me to find you. And I… I can't ever find you."

"I'm okay, now. I'm here. I'm right here with you, Ben," Pete whispered into Ben's hair.

Ben's tears slowed as Pete continued to chant over and over again, "I'm fine, baby. I'm here. I'm here with you."

"I just need you. I need you, Pete."

"I'm here, Ben. Always."

Pete hoped the rest of the night would pass without more tears, without more aching. But there were more. Pete wept as Ben came inside him, overcome with the emotions of the pleasure coursing through him, the steady and clear light in Ben's eyes looking up at him. Ben broke down when Pete kissed his shoulder—just like he used to.

They were just curling around each other again, drifting off to sleep, when suddenly, Pete wrenched his head away from Ben's shoulder, peering at the sky. A faint whine in the sky grew louder.

Pete jumped up and slipped on his pants with practiced ease.

"Ben, get dressed." Pete's voice held an authority and command Ben had never heard before. "We need to go. Now."

"What…" Ben struggled into his shirt as Pete jammed his feet in his boots. "What's going on?"

"We need to get back to base, on the double."

"What? Why?" Ben's pants were half-fastened, as he crammed his feet in his shoes.

Pete reached his hand out blindly to help him up, his attention already back on the sky.

"Those aren't our planes."

CHAPTER ELEVEN

THEY RAN FASTER THAN BEN thought possible, dodging trees and jumping over bushes, the loud buzzing drone of the enemy planes growing louder with each step. When the camp was just in sight, they heard the ear-blasting whine of the air raid siren begin.

Pete, his face set and grim, pulled Ben back as they were about to burst into the meadow surrounding the base's airfield. He crouched at the tree line, pulling Ben down to safety next to him, just as the first enemy planes flew over them. They dropped flares to mark their targets, eye-searingly bright against the dark night sky.

Pete watched the camp intently. The men boiled from barracks and buildings, some sprinting to their posts, others sprinting towards their planes.

"Benjamin, we are going to run now." Pete looked seriously into Ben's eyes. "I need you right behind me—you do everything I do, okay?"

Ben was trembling—desperately trying to keep his panic from showing. He never knew airplanes could be so loud, or that gunfire would make your ears go deaf. He swore he was feeling the noises in his bones.

Pete took his cold, shaking hands in his own—Pete's hands were calm and steady and warm.

"Okay, B?" Pete's voice softened, a smile touching his eyes. "I need you with me."

Heartened, Ben swallowed hard, and nodded.

"I'm going to get you to headquarters—that's the safest place for you—but then I'm going to have to get The Redhead off the ground before she gets hit." Pete's voice was steady, with a note of command Ben had never heard before.

I'd follow him anywhere—it doesn't matter where, Ben thought as he nodded again.

"But we have to get you there before the bombers arrive. This is a squadron of fighters; their bombers won't be too far behind."

Ben nodded frantically, eyes wide.

"Are you ready to run?" Pete was still looking intently at Ben, though his body was quivering with adrenaline.

"Wait." Ben surged forward for one last passionate kiss, capturing Pete's lips with his own.

"I love you," Pete breathed into his mouth.

"I love you, too."

"Ready?"

Ben nodded.

"You stay right behind me, okay, baby?"

At Ben's nod, Pete grabbed his hand. They stood and ran like hell, bullets flying all around them.

Pete sprinted between obstacles, dragging Ben behind, ducking them behind posts and into doorways as they made their way across the base; bullets from the enemy planes sprayed all around them.

A loud whine from nearby, then a choking sputter, and Ben could see one—or maybe three or four—smaller planes taxiing to the runway.

Pete glanced up as they took off. "Good. Joe's up. George, Tommy— good, that's good," he muttered.

He took another deep breath, squeezed Ben's hand and ran to the next building.

Ben heard the zing and pop of the bullets and felt gravel spray up from the shots that missed them stinging his skin.

As soon as the strafing run began, Pete ran, seeming to chase the bullets. Ben hesitated a fraction of a second before Pete grabbed his hand and pulled. "These planes can't fire behind them. It's safer to go now."

Ben tried to stop thinking, instead just following Pete. *Follow Pete, stay with Pete, stay with him.*

"One more, baby, one more," Pete promised as they reached the safety of the next doorway. The door behind them suddenly opened—Charlie was just about to spring out. He grabbed Pete around the waist with one arm, ready to drag him out towards their plane.

"We gotta go, Cap'n. We gotta go! They're sitting ducks out there!" Charlie's voice was high.

"I'll be right there, Charlie. I'm gonna get him inside, then I'll be there. Get everybody ready to go up."

"Yes sir." Charlie spun around, his boots crunching in the gravel and sprinted off into the murky darkness.

Pete pushed Ben in front of him, making one last dash.

The body-shaking low drone increased as the first bombers came into sight. Pete shoved Ben through the door, into safety, as the first bomb exploded behind him.

* * *

When the first enemy planes were spotted, Gwen and her crew were hastily escorted to headquarters, where they sat huddled against the wall, trying to keep out of the way as the world exploded around them. Radio operators rapidly gave out orders, speaking tensely into their headsets, relaying information from soldiers and pilots and planes not quite ready. The air raid siren continued sounding; boots pounded outside during the lulls.

Gwen and the pilot of her tour plane stood with the base commander, mulling over options.

"I don't think we have enough time to get your plane safely away before the rest of this flight wing arrives," the commander said shortly. "I know you've got a red cross on your plane, but we can't ever guarantee that they're gonna honor that."

"Then we stay." Gwen decided. "Thank you, sir, and we'll do our best to stay out of your way."

"Thank you, Miss Andrews."

Gwen turned smartly, planning how best to tell her entourage they were about to experience their very first air raid. She hoped this would be nothing like the newsreels she'd seen of the bombings on London.

Ginger pushed her way through the door. She was helping the other nurses move patients from the hospital to the more heavily fortified and secure headquarters.

"Red," Gwen called to her. "Give my girls something to do."

Ginger pointed out several patients. "Just hold their hands, talk to them. Keep them with you."

Gwen sat down between two soldiers who were already in treatment for shock. She took their hands—theirs were cold and clammy, and she wasn't sure that hers were much better. Still, it felt better to hold on to someone.

"Keep them warm and go overboard on the light chit-chat," Ginger whispered to her. "Just try to keep their minds from what's going on outside."

Ginger sped off to help the rest of the medical crew prepare for more soldiers—the wounded who would inevitably come.

Gwen could hear the radio operators speaking in low monotones to the planes and pilots. Most of it sounded like gibberish, but she did hear a voice advising that the Riveting Redhead still did not have a full crew and were waiting for Montgomery.

Oh God, Pete and Ben are still out there. She went cold. There were no windows, but Gwen could feel the percussion of the bombs through the wall at her back.

The door burst open again, two figures silhouetted against the firestorm outside.

One figure shoved the other inside: Ben, who nearly stumbled and fell over the threshold.

Pete's attention was drawn immediately outside, back to something Gwen, and Ben, couldn't see. He spun to look inside once more, and caught sight of Gwen.

"Gwen! Please!" Pete screamed over the thunderous bursts outside. "Get him out of here!"

He turned to launch himself towards the flight line, slamming the door shut behind him.

Ben's legs finally gave out and he slumped to the floor.

Over the din of so many voices over the radio, the operators on the ground speaking in low monotones, the pilots and crews shouting, Ben could pick out Pete's voice: mostly calm, sometimes rising in pitch as he detailed their movements—*evasive maneuvers, stall, restart*—

Ben couldn't keep still. His leg bounced; he chewed his lip; he cracked his knuckles. He was going mad, sitting here, not being able to *do* anything. It was still dark, still a few hours from dawn. The sandbags dampened the sounds from outside, and the room crackled with nervous energy. A few soldiers rushed through the door, carrying a wounded man slung between their soldiers, barely able to walk themselves, blood streaming down their faces. The nurses flew into action, helping wounded men get settled and patched up.

A shortwave radio crackled from a box on the floor near Ben, ignored by everyone else in the frantic HQ.

"Hello? Please, is there anybody there? Hello?"

Ben scrambled to grab the handset from the box, fumbling in his haste. It sounded like a little girl speaking.

"Hello? Yes? I'm here," he said softly into it.

"Could you perhaps help me, please?" the little voice whispered. "I should like to go home."

"Absolutely, darling." Gwen leaned against Ben's shoulder, speaking soothingly into the radio. "We can help you."

"Oh, thank goodness." The little girl started to cry, babbling. "Mummy said I could see the famous American's show and said I must be a very good girl afterwards and go right to sleep, but it's so loud outside now and I can't find anyone. I'm so frightened about the bombs. Mum said last week it's the Jerries, come to kill us all, and I just don't want to die today."

"Oh, darling, no, hush," Gwen cooed. "You're not going to die today. Tell us where you are, and we'll come help you."

"I'm at the motor pond. Please come quickly."

"Of course, love. How old are you, darling?"

"I'm nearly six," she lisped precisely. "I've lost three teeth already!"

Ben handed the radio to Gwen and shot up, sprinting over to the desks where radio operators were still grimly helping the base's airplanes in their fight. "There's a little girl here; she's found a radio. She says she's at the motor pond and she's asking us for help."

The commanding officer's face blanched as he heaved a sigh. "That must be Daisy Swan. A little girl from the village; her mother works in the laundry. But I heard she's been ill. She sent Daisy here with a neighbor to see the show last night. Daisy means the motor pool, not the pond. It's over on the east corner of the compound."

"That's not far, right? We have to go get her," Ben stated.

The officer darted his eyes around the room. "No, it's not far, but look, we've all got our hands full here. I don't have enough men, and everyone else is pinned down, spread out across the base for the duration. I don't have anyone to spare."

Ben couldn't say anything; his stomach was knotted in shock.

"Fuck." The officer viciously kicked a nearby trashcan under the desk. "Daisy's a sweetheart—her dad's off in the army and it's just her and her mum. But I just can't—"

"I'll go," Ben decided. "I'll go find her and get her somewhere safe."

"I can't authorize you—"

"I'm not under your authority. I'm going out there and if I get myself killed trying to save a terrified child, then it's my own goddamned fault. But I'm not just going to leave her out there in this."

"—Thank you," the officer looked relieved. "Daisy's a good girl, and we all are fond of her—"

"I'll find her safe."

Ginger spoke seriously with a few soldiers, before marching over with another radio. She clapped a steel helmet on his head and tossed a musette bag with medical supplies in it over his shoulder, just in case.

"Keep your wits about you, you fool," she ordered. "Don't start getting cocky thinking that it's over and do something stupid."

"Yes, ma'am." He grinned. "I'll be back before you know it."

By the door, Gwen was still cooing at the child through the radio, keeping her calm as best she could.

"Daisy, darling girl? My friend Benny is coming to help you, all right darling? Just stay right where you are, and he'll be there faster than you can say 'Jack Robinson.'"

"Jack Robinson." Daisy giggled.

"Hey now," Ben tested out his radio, teasing. "You need to give me a fair start!"

"That's Ben, darling girl," Gwen cooed, again.

"Hullo, Ben," Daisy said quietly.

"Hello, Daisy." Ben smiled despite the danger, crouching at the door to peer out at the chaos outside: fires burning, bright flashes of bombs exploding. "Now, Daisy girl, you need to help me here. I'm not from around here, so you need to tell me exactly where you are."

"Oh, I'm in Mr. Thompson's office," Daisy relayed. "He's in charge of the jeeps. He gives me a lift back to the village sometimes when he goes in to see Miss Duddlesworth. He says she's got nice buns."

Ben choked back a startled laugh, unsure if Miss Duddlesworth had a tea shop, or a shapely backside. He counted to three, took a deep breath and slipped out the door into the sudden silence outside, heading in a straight shot down the lane toward the motor pool. It looked a lot farther away than it had on his tour of the base.

"Okay, Daisy," he heard Gwen reporting. "Ben is on his way."

"How will I know it's him?" Daisy asked. "Mum says I mustn't speak to strangers."

I'm the only one coming to find you in the middle of an air raid, he thought, wryly.

"Oh, well, darling," Gwen drawled dramatically. "He's incredibly handsome, like a movie star."

"Like Clark Gable?" Daisy sounded breathless, but at least she no longer sounded frightened.

"Oh, no. More like… Gary Cooper. Do you know him?"

"No." Over Ben's radio, Daisy didn't sound impressed. He was a third of the way toward the motor pool, kicking up gravel as he sprinted recklessly. He heard the distant whine of planes approaching.

"Oh, Daisy darling." It sounded as if Gwen and Daisy were girlfriends gossiping over a cup of coffee. "He's tall and lithe and handsome. Blue eyes, blond hair. Makes you weak in the knees."

"What does 'lithe' mean, Miss Gwen?"

Ben heard the metallic popping of bullets in the distance as the enemy planes made another strafing run ahead of their bombers. As they got closer, he threw himself inside the nearest door, slamming it shut and flattening himself against it. His stomach roiled, his hands were shaking but he grabbed the radio and interrupted them, speaking urgently.

"Daisy, there's another line of planes coming," he said firmly. "Get under the desk, or somewhere where you're not out in the open, and stay put. I'm on my way to get you."

"Yes, Ben," she said, in a small frightened voice. "Please do hurry."

He took another deep breath and hurled his way out the door, sprinting from doorway to doorway as the next round of bombs began to hit behind him. He threw himself through the open side of the building that was the motor pool, tuning in again on Gwen's rising panic over the radio.

"Daisy? Daisy! Come on, love, talk to me. You need to talk to me so we can help Ben find you, darling."

Ben's stomach went stone-cold with fear that he wouldn't be able to find her in the murky black inside the building. Out of the corner of his eye, he saw a blur of movement, shadows moving in the blackness. An explosion outside lit the interior brightly and he saw one little blue shoe, battered and worn under the desk in the corner.

"Daisy," he called softly, dropping to his knees. "Daisy, little love? It's Ben. I'm here to take you to see Miss Gwen."

A little pale face, golden hair falling out of two braids, poked out suddenly from beneath the desk as Daisy began to crawl towards him. She went straight into his arms, curling up and bursting into tears. "I want my mum."

"We'll get you to her, love, just as soon as we can. Right now, we're going to see Miss Gwen, where it's going to be safe and everything's going to be all right."

"I don't want to go out there, Ben," she wailed.

"But, we need to go out there. It's not safe here." *Not with the gas tanks of the jeeps just waiting to explode into fireballs*, he thought.

"Please don't make me go." She burrowed deeper into his arms.

"Baby girl, come on," he cajoled. "We can do it."

"I'm not a baby!" She glared at him, suddenly fierce, hiccupping through her tears.

"Daisy, darling," Gwen's voice came over the radio. "Daisy, you know, I have a shade of lipstick here that I think will be just perfect on a young lady such as yourself."

Gwen, you're an angel, Ben thought.

"And Ben's friend Ginger says she's been saving a chocolate bar to share with someone special, and she says you can have the bigger piece once you get here."

"Ginger usually has very good chocolate," Ben said, seriously. The bombs falling outside rumbled through the ground beneath their feet. She nodded and wrapped her arms around his neck. He tightened his arms around her and lifted her up, heading for the door as quickly as he could.

"Okay, Daisy," he said, looking out the door again. "This is it. We're just gonna run as fast as we can."

"I can't run very fast," she said doubtfully into his shoulder.

"Well, no, darling. I'm going to carry you. You hold on tight and I'll run."

BEN BURST THROUGH THE DOOR, the terrified little girl cradled in his arms, her face buried in his chest. Gwen reached to take her from him as he dropped to the floor to catch his breath and calm his pounding heart. They checked her over carefully for any injuries, but aside from a few scratches, she seemed perfectly fine.

They kept her busy to keep her mind, and their minds, off the bombing. One of the wounded soldiers made her a doll out of a bandage and some cotton batting, which she cradled in her arms and cooed over. Babbling all the while, she piled up the spare blankets they'd found her, stuffing them underneath a desk to make herself a nest. Still jabbering away, she curled up in her nest and promptly fell asleep, the ragdoll clutched in her arms.

With Daisy safe and asleep, Ben sat with his back against the wall, near Gwen and her patients. They started one of their scripted show banters, managing to distract the men around them, at least for a short time. Gwen told a funny story of growing up in Savannah, drawling out her words theatrically and winking.

Ben could see Gwen's nervousness underneath the polished shell and how quickly her eyes darted over the room when she thought no one was looking. The room was piled high with sandbags; the windows were completely blocked. The room was lit by a few bare light bulbs—tense and very claustrophobic. The wounded soldiers clutched her hands tightly, and she smiled to reassure them.

They noticed when the explosions seemed to slow. No more gunfire. Just one final loud percussion, then nothing.

"I think it's over." Gwen smiled broadly, patting at the soldier's legs near her. "See, boys? Nothing to worry about."

She stood to check that everyone else was okay.

Ben's ears were ringing with the absence of sound. He couldn't hear the loud ticking until it abruptly stopped.

"Benny?" Gwen turned back to face him, a smile on her face, as the wall behind her exploded in shards of white and flame.

* * *

THE FIRST TIME BEN OPENED his eyes, all he could see was dust flying, backlit by red. He tried to take in a deep breath, and was rewarded with a lungful of searing debris. He choked and tried to roll to his side, but something kept him flat on his back.

Through the dust, he could see a man lying near him—Hugo the drummer, he thought—a man whose eyes were streaming, his face contorted in agony, his mouth wide in what must be a scream. But Ben couldn't hear it.

He couldn't hear it, and his entire body jolted with panic as he reached up to brush away whatever was covering his ears. A sharp burning pain in his leg overwhelmed him. His vision flashed to blinding white and he passed back into unconsciousness.

The second time Ben opened his eyes, the dust had settled. Through the dark, he could see what must be flashlight beams of people moving towards him.

He turned his head to look for the man next to him, but the man had turned his face away. After a few seconds, Ben realized he wasn't sure if the man was still breathing.

Ben thought this should bother him—thought he should do something to help. But he started to feel chilly; the only warmth was on his legs—which were still pinned to the ground. His arms felt heavy and useless. He calmly watched the lights coming closer to him. He wished they'd bring him a blanket. He closed his eyes again.

The next time Ben opened his eyes, it was involuntarily. Someone flashed a bright light at his left eye, while roughly pulling up his eyelid. Ben wanted to tell them that hurt. But his tongue was heavy and thick in his mouth.

The person behind the light nodded—he could see her mouth moving but no sound came out. She raised her head, mouth open wider as if calling to someone.

She looked back down at him, her face smudged with dirt and ash and blood. She smiled reassuringly at him, and Ben tried to smile back. She patted him on the shoulder, then looked up to greet whoever just arrived to help.

Ben wondered why he felt so detached, so dispassionate. He still felt cold. He could feel grit in his eyes. His fingers and hands were heavy and tingling. He definitely could not hear and he definitely could not move his legs. He thought he should be more upset, but he couldn't summon the energy.

Dimly, he was aware of someone grabbing his hand. He turned his head to find himself staring, however improbably, into the wide, anxious, golden eyes of Pete.

Pete was holding his hand, gripping it tightly, Ben thought, because that's just how Pete was.

Ben felt—he finally felt—a rush of panic. He needed to make Pete understand that he couldn't hear—knew Pete would understand why that's important, would understand because Pete always understands him.

Ben was breathing in short pants; his mouth was so dry and full of dust that he choked.

* * *

THE PROPELLERS OF THE RIVETING Redhead had barely slowed when Pete started frantically unbuckling his straps, flipping final switches.

"You go find him," Jim said quietly, interrupting him. "I'll make sure she's good and parked, then I'll be right behind you."

Pete sucked in a breath to say thank you, but instead nodded shortly. Jim nodded in return. No need for words.

He vaulted from the cockpit and out of the plane. He joined the straggle of men leaping from their planes, pelting their way across the airfield towards what was left of their base.

Pete barely recognized the HQ when he arrived there—what was a small brick building was now a twisted pile of smoking metal and rubble. A small child sat on the ground in a cleared spot, face dirty with soot, hair straggling out of two braids and solemnly sucking her thumb. Next to her, he saw Ginger, already at work, her green fatigues soaked with blood at the knees, her red hair pulled severely back out of her way. She had a cut on her neck that was still oozing blood. She impatiently swiped at it with some gauze in one hand as she crouched to take the pulse of the soldier lying in front of her.

"It's all right, Daisy girl," Ginger explained calmly to the little girl. "This soldier here just got a bad knock on the head. His pulse is good, his color's good, he's not bleeding. It's like he's gone to sleep for a bit, but he'll wake up in no time. He'll probably have a great big headache, though."

The little girl giggled quietly, reassured for the moment, and Ginger smiled at her, before moving to the next soldier.

Pete grabbed the gauze from her startled fingers, spread it over the cut and firmly applied pressure to stop the bleeding. He was impressed with how steady his hands were, despite the frantic hammering of his heart.

"Ben?" His voice was anything but steady. He fought to keep calm, to think rationally, choking back panic.

"He's here. Somewhere," Ginger gestured at the ruins in front of them. "I was busy with other things so I wasn't watching him when it hit—but I'm pretty sure he and Gwen and the rest are over there." She pointed at the far corner.

"So we've got to clear our way from here to there." Pete sucked in a deep breath and coughed at the acrid air. "Okay, let's go then."

He jumped right in, following behind the doctors and nurses moving over the wreckage, shifting and pulling debris out of the way, carrying wounded to safer areas. He always kept an eye on where they thought Ben might be, always working towards it, across the shortest distance to Ben.

He had just reached a nurse kneeling beside a man she needed help moving when he heard a shout behind him.

"That wall's not stable! It's coming down!"

Pete launched himself across the wounded man, grabbing the nurse's shoulders and tucking her head against his chest. He braced himself not to fall directly on the ground as the wall collapsed on top of them; bits of metal and brick bounced off his shoulders and back instead of directly into their faces.

Another impromptu corpsman came to help; they shifted the rubble and the wounded man was carried off.

Benjamin. Ben, Ben, oh God, where's Ben.

He couldn't stop now.

CHAPTER TWELVE

IRENE, THE NURSE WHO'D TAKEN a fancy to him at the dance, was kneeling next to someone—maybe even a pile of people, judging from the number of splayed limbs in front of her.

"Corpsmen! I need some help over here!"

Pete scrambled closer, over the piles of rubble as he recognized that forehead—that chin he'd kissed so many times. Those lips. Benjamin.

Ben's eyes blinked slowly and Pete had a flash of thankfulness Irene was in the way so he was unable to throw himself down and kiss every available inch of him.

Pete darted his eyes over Ben, searching for injury. He saw blood oozing down from Ben's ears, not surprising given how close he'd been to the bomb when it went off. Some blood was already drying in his hair. He raked his eyes down. Ben was covered in rubble from the waist down.

The other corpsmen began to excavate him, gently pulling rock and metal away from his legs.

One of them eyed the pile of rubble doubtfully. "Can he sit up? We might be able to pull him out instead of moving all this stuff."

Irene and Pete put their arms behind Ben's shoulders and pulled him up to a sitting position. Ben's eyes briefly closed as a wave of dizziness hit him. But almost instantly, they popped open, searching frantically until he found Pete again.

Pete knelt down next to him, supporting his shoulders. Ben's lips trembled. Pete could see tears in his eyes. He pressed their foreheads together, whispering, "It's okay, it's okay now. You're okay. I've got you. I'm here. Stay with me, baby. It's okay."

BEN THOUGHT HIS HEARING MIGHT be returning, impossibly slowly. Instead of the shocking absence of sound, he started to hear low rumbles, from far away—as if he was underwater. He turned his head, resting his forehead against Pete's cheek. He could just see Pete's lips—those rosy, full, deliciously kissable lips that he's been dreaming of.

Because he'd spent a lifetime, surely, of looking at Pete's lips, watching them in every expression of emotion, in every laze of sleep, he could tell what Pete was saying over and over again.

"I've got you, baby. It's okay. I've got you."

Ben's mind wandered. He knew what those words looked like in Pete's mouth, because he'd seen them before—the first time he cried in front of Pete. His father had had an attack of some sort; he'd been blue at the lips and gasping and collapsed. His sister could barely speak when she'd telephoned Ben in New York to tell him. Ben had gone numb with shock, absolutely numb, even though his dad had woken up and was grumbling good-naturedly and the doctors had said he'd need to be cautious, but he'd recover. Ben had been numb to everything, until Pete had passed by him in the kitchen and gently wrapped his arm around Ben's waist—Ben seized hold of him, kissing him wildly. He could feel again.

But it wasn't until they were in bed, Ben demanding and begging and asking for Pete, however whenever Pete wanted—it wasn't until Pete was moving strongly inside him that he cried, sobbing as the shell enclosing his heart shattered. Pete had wanted to stop, but Ben begged him to keep going.

So, Pete had leaned close, his lips so close to Ben's, their foreheads almost touching.

"I've got you, baby. It's okay. I've got you."

THE CORPSMEN WERE BACK TO shifting the rubble. Something was stuck on Ben's legs and they couldn't pull him out.

Pete was watching Ben—Ben's fair skin looking beyond pale, waxy and nearly gray. Sweat was beading on Ben's nose, on his forehead, and Pete tried to find something to wipe it away.

Then, from beneath the rubble, he saw a flash of hair. Red hair. Gwen's hair.

Oh God, Gwen.

BEN LEANED HEAVILY ON PETE, panting shallowly. Nauseated, his mind whirled. He couldn't believe Pete was safe, Pete was sitting next to him. He could smell him—his aftershave nearly lost beneath the sharp scent of sweat and fear, but so very Pete. Pete was here. His mind grasped that before spiraling off into nothingness again.

The corpsmen were frantically scrabbling in the rubble. They found two soldiers at the edge of the pile, stunned and trapped.

Ben's attention was drawn to the men working to pull the large piece of metal that had his legs pinned. As they wrenched it out of the way, Pete let out a loud moan.

Ben didn't understand his reaction. That was not one of the moans he usually heard from Pete, moans between gasping breaths of pleasure, or the quiet moans when he'd been ill. This was... Ben didn't know what that sound was.

Ben didn't know why he still couldn't move his legs. His eyes flitted down to them, tried to discover what's wrong. He didn't understand—he couldn't understand—why someone had laid a very large piece of meat, bloody and raw, across his legs. He tried to hold hard to the thought before his mind flitted away again. He just wished they'd move it so he could get out of here and Pete could hold him properly.

When he recognized the hair fanning out, he realized the piece of meat was all that is left of Gwen Andrews.

He began to scream and couldn't stop.

"OH CHRIST." PETE CHOKED BACK a wave of nausea, holding Ben tightly, burying Ben's screams in his shoulder. The corpsmen gently moved Gwen's body out of the way, wrapping a blanket around her, covering her face.

"Gwen!" Ben's voice was too loud and full of panic. "Pete!"

"Shh, Ben. Shh." Pete wrapped his arms around him tightly, scooting closer to him to hold him down. Ben, his legs now free, tried to rise, tried to get to Gwen—Pete held him back.

Pete was suddenly aware of a hot pulsing on his own leg and looked down, astonished, to see blood spurting from a wound in Ben's leg.

"Help!" Pete yelled, clamping his hand down on Ben's leg.

Irene sprinted across to him, clamping her own hand on top of his. "Femoral artery. Keep that pressure on—hard—or he's going to bleed out in a matter of minutes."

Pete grabbed Ben's leg viciously tight. Ben's color went entirely gray as he passed out.

"Let's go, boys!" Irene helped the corpsmen hurl Ben onto a stretcher. "Surgery. Now!"

Pete desperately kept his hold on Ben's thigh, running along with the stretcher in the thin and watery early morning light toward the hospital, holding Ben's very life in his hand.

CHAPTER THIRTEEN

IT WAS HOT UP IN the hayloft. It was hot everywhere, really, but in the hayloft, half-empty with just the season's first cut of hay, it was very hot. The sunlight blazed through the open loft door, and when Ben half-opened his eyes, he could see bits of dust from the hay dancing lazily around, almost sparkling.

They were beautiful, sparkling, but not as beautiful as the sparks in Robert's blue eyes. Robert was propped on one elbow, looking down into Ben's face, kissing him gently. Ben lifted his head slightly, straining to meet Robert's lips, as the nervous butterflies in his stomach slowly moved farther down his body, coalescing just underneath Robert's hand moving in Ben's trousers.

Robert unbuttoned the fly slowly—Ben had always hated those trousers with their tiny buttons—exposing his hand, and Ben, to the warm air. They both shook, clumsy with unaccustomed want and need.

This is wrong; they told me this is wrong, this is wrong, but oh God, oh God, please oh God, don't stop, it can't be wrong, oh God it can't be.

Suddenly, there was too much air in the room. Ben's head was spinning and he couldn't breathe with all the air and light around him and he didn't know if he wanted to laugh or cry, but he awkwardly jerked his hips once, twice into Robert's hand, and his entire body filled with warmth and joy and light.

They shared a shy, trembling kiss that was quickly broken when Ben heard his father's voice calling from the dooryard below.

"Ben! You in here?" his dad's voice was definitely just downstairs, just outside the barn door.

"Oh my God." Both boys scrambled to their feet, Ben wiping his stomach with his shirttail, awkwardly pulling up his pants, then hurriedly shuffling towards the ladder.

He couldn't leave like this, though. He turned back, smiling into Pete's face, momentarily confused when his first sweetheart was gone and Pete was there instead. But his heart soared when he saw the answering smile in Pete's golden eyes.

"Tomorrow?" Ben whispered. His smile widened when Pete nodded shyly.

"Okay," Ben said, giggling as he leaned for a kiss, "because I really have to go now, or my dad's going to kill us both."

"Ben, you don't have to—" Pete mumbled.

"Shhhh, tomorrow, we'll do it again. For you." Ben could hardly speak for giggling, couldn't believe how forward and brave he felt, couldn't believe that he kissed a boy—a boy—here in the hayloft with his father just beginning to bellow below him.

With one last peck on Pete's lips, Ben started down the ladder, turning and swinging to grab the floor joist with both hands to drop himself to floor—as he'd done countless times before.

Except countless times before, he hadn't been loose-limbed and giddy, and he hadn't been buzzing with his first-ever orgasm caused by someone else, someone who thought he was wonderful and kissed like a dream; and his fifteen-year-old body didn't recall that the floor was a lot farther down than he thought. He landed awkwardly, heard a loud snapping crunch and rolled to the floor, gasping at the pain and clutching his knee. His knee would never be the same.

"Ben!" Pete's voice was louder now, and Ben wanted to tell him he has to get back, back, back up in the hayloft before his dad sees him, because then he'll suspect. And then suddenly, they were in the dairy of his father's farm; Pete was carrying in two heavy buckets of fresh milk and winking at Ben as he sat churning butter.

BEN HAD A VERY SERIOUS conversation with the man who taught him mathematics when he was seventeen, but he couldn't remember what it was about. He thought it might be about geometry, but the shapes were all so pretty that he got distracted, especially when they started floating around him.

THE ALARM CLOCK WAS RINGING, ringing, ringing, and Ben moaned for Pete to turn it off. Pete wasn't in bed, though, and Ben had to whack at the bedside table in order to find it and flick the switch before the damn bell silenced.

Ben buried his head back in his pillow. His head was pounding, his ass was aching, and he only had a vague recollection of leaving the party the night before. He remembered going out to the supper club, Bets excited and chattering over a new role, toasting everyone with champagne. He thought he remembered dancing with Bets—dear God, he hoped it was Bets—and trying to remember had just made him nauseous, and his head hurt like hell, so he tried to stop.

Ben knew Pete was there by the way the bed shifted as he sat down next to him.

"Rise and shine, sleepyhead," Pete gently teased. "I brought you coffee."

Ben groaned. "You are an angel and I love you."

Pete laughed. "I love you too." He smoothed a hand over Ben's wild hair as Ben struggled to sit up enough to sip at the steaming mug Pete handed him.

"Why the fuck did you let me drink so much?"

Pete groaned and dropped his head into his hands. "Well, we were doing okay until they brought out the champagne."

"Oh, baby. And champagne always knocks you on your ass." Ben nodded—slightly—in sympathy.

"And champagne always knocks me on my ass, that's right. I was in no shape to curtail your drinking."

"I'm sorry, baby."

"I'm sorry, too."

"WHAT DO YOU HAVE TO be sorry for, baby?" Pete's hoarse whisper was confused.

"The… the champagne. I'm sorry for the champagne."

Pete chuckled quietly in the dark. He'd been sitting next to Ben's bed since they brought him out of surgery, shifting uncomfortably when too much of his weight rested on his shoulder. He squinted at his watch, radium-painted hands and numbers glowing in the dimness: not quite two a.m.

He wasn't sure what Ben was dreaming this time; Ben hadn't actually regained full consciousness for longer than a minute. Pete thought the fact that he mumbled and muttered and was clearly dreaming was a good sign. Pete had always loved that Ben talked in his sleep. Back home, there had been so many silly moments, conversations they'd had, Pete not knowing Ben was asleep, his dreamy, silly, beautiful Ben. Here, he'd had to speak sharply to Ben at times, to keep him from revealing too much when there were too many people around. But now, in the middle of the night, in the dark, they could whisper to each other and it was almost like being back home, together, before all of this hurt and pain and anguish happened. If only Ben would wake up.

Pete wrapped his hand more securely around Ben's and tried to resettle himself enough to go back to sleep.

BILL WENT DUTIFULLY INTO THE hospital ward to have the bandages on his hands changed. He'd sliced them helping extricate other survivors from the HQ rubble and, though he didn't like to admit it, they hurt like the dickens.

With his hands freshly bandaged, he snuck onto the ward where he knew the Captain had been keeping vigil at his cousin's bedside. He's the one who'd come up with that story, after all—the whole "cousins" thing was a ruse, because as soon as he'd seen the two of them in a room together, he'd known. They had eyes only for each other, and it tugged at something in his chest to see it. He'd had that with his Marjorie. People had said they could just tell he and Marjorie were in love; from a million miles away, they could see it.

He was quiet when he came around the corner and he saw Pete asleep, sitting up in a chair with his arm strapped tightly and painfully to his chest, scruffy and disheveled, still in blood-stained clothes. Bill knew Pete wouldn't leave Ben's bedside for anything less than the absolute essentials. Bill remembered that, too.

Just a small, pained noise from Ben, still asleep, and Pete's eyes flew open. He leaned over Ben's pillow, brushing the hair off Ben's forehead, anxiously watching for any other signs of distress.

"It's okay, baby," Pete whispered. "You're okay. It's okay, now."

When there was no response, Pete settled his chair a little closer to the bed and tried to find a comfortable position for his hurt arm that would still allow him to hold Ben's hand. He sighed heavily, and was asleep again.

Bill watched him, watched the two of them, feeling a tightness around his chest. The determination in Pete's face, the fierceness with which he held Ben's hand, as if declaring that anyone or anything who tried to come and take him away would have to get through Pete first—Bill remembered that, too.

That's how he'd held Marjorie's hand, that godawful summer the baby came too early. She'd fought so hard and bled so much, and he'd held her hand through it all, and there hadn't been anything anyone could do. And he'd still been holding her hand when she'd slipped away.

Bill backed away, as quietly as he could. He sent up a prayer to— to anyone who'll listen. Maybe they'd listen, this time.

Please don't take him.

BEN WAS HOT. HE WAS so hot he could feel sweat beading on his upper lip and behind his kneecaps.

"I swear to God, Pete, I think my fingernails are sweating."

Pete laughed beside him, that wonderfully sexy deep rumble in his chest. August in the city was scorching. They'd kept their window shades drawn all day, keeping out the blazing sun. With night fallen, they'd thrown everything open in the hope of catching even the slightest breeze.

They were laying on their backs, side-by-side on their bed, completely nude, arms and legs slightly spread like starfish, endeavoring to be close without actually touching, letting the meager air from their fan play over their bodies.

"Do you know, Pete?" Ben murmured. "I think this is the very first time I've had you naked beside me without having absolutely *any* desire to fuck you."

"Shhh, Ben," Pete whispered. "Shhh, darling, not now."

Ben went back to contemplating Pete's naked body—or at least what he could see of it without raising his head. Pete was glistening with sweat wherever the breeze from the fan didn't reach, making his lusciously tanned skin glow in the moonlight, glimmer like gold: twenty-four-karat gold, like a diamond necklace.

Or maybe it was his mother's locket. *Where was that locket? Did his father have it in a box somewhere, or did he give it to—*

"Hey." Pete brought his thoughts back from wandering. "Squeeze my hand, will you?"

Ben didn't remember taking Pete's hand. He was almost certain they'd sworn not to even touch fingertips because of the heat.

"Why?" Ben asked.

"I just need to know you're okay before I can sleep."

At dawn the next day, Ben finally woke up. Pete was asleep, sitting up in a straight-backed chair, his feet propped on the end of Ben's bed. His head lolled back against the wall behind him; his face was bearded with what must be several days' stubble.

Ben watched him for a moment; he looked exhausted, even while sleeping. There was a gash on his forehead and a bruise on his cheekbone, and his left arm was strapped tightly to his side. His uniform was absolutely filthy—stained dark brown all over.

At the slight shift in Ben's breathing, Pete's eyes snapped open, instantly leaning forward toward Ben, brushing the hair off of Ben's forehead with his good hand.

"Red?" He said quietly but firmly, as he looked steadily into Ben's eyes.

A shuffling out of Ben's line of sight, gentle footsteps, and then Ginger came into view.

She quickly took his vitals, giving both him and Pete a reassuring smile.

"See? What did I tell you, Petey? Nothing to worry about."

Pete chuckled, without humor. "Uh-huh."

Ginger bent closer to Ben, peering into his face. "Jesus, Benjamin. You look like hell!"

Ben's eyes widened.

"You're starting to look like your great-aunt Gertrude." She squinted at him, gauging his reaction.

Ben narrowed his eyes, raised an eyebrow and glared at her.

"See?" She gestured with one hand towards Ben's face. "Practically back to normal."

Pete laughed quietly at Ben's expression.

"Water?" Ben croaked. His mouth was so dry.

Ginger nodded, poured him a small cup and helped him sip it.

Pete sat back in his chair, sighing. He used his right arm to shift his left arm to an easier position and scratched at the skin underneath the edge of the bandage.

"Hey now. You leave that alone, Montgomery," Ginger said slapping his hand. "You dislodge my text-book perfect strapping and there's going to be hell to pay."

"Aren't you a nurse? Are you supposed to have sympathy or empathy for all creatures, or something?" Pete pretended to complain.

"General sympathy, yes. Sympathy for idiots who purposefully throw themselves under collapsing walls, no."

"What?" Ben's hearing was still muddled, and he wasn't quite sure he'd heard this correctly.

"This numbskull here," Ginger said, jerking her thumb toward Pete, "went and tossed me out of the way when a wall—an entire wall—was coming down, but didn't get himself out of the way in time."

"Red, you know I had to—"

"—And that was the *second* wall he'd been under in the space of a few hours. Thinks he's a damned Knight in Shining Armor, I imagine."

"I know he is," Ben said quietly.

From down the darkened ward, a loud moan, followed by a plea of "Nurse!" Ginger looked Ben over one last time, and pointed a finger at Pete, admonishing.

"You let him know what's going on? And remember, shift change—such as it is—will be in twenty minutes, and the next head nurse isn't all sweetness and light, like me, so you won't be able to put your feet up on the bed anymore."

She hurried off down the ward, muttering something about "damned stupid hospital corners in the bed sheets."

"What… what happened?"

"First things, first. We need to keep you calm, okay? The blast ripped open a very important vein—or artery, or something—something really important—and they were able to repair it so you didn't bleed to death—.

Pete closed his eyes against the memory of clutching Ben's leg as tightly as he could and running along with the stretcher toward the makeshift hospital, so much blood spilling so fast between his fingers *is this tight enough, oh God please let this be enough, please, please, oh fucking please, don't let this happen, please let him be okay,* Ben's face growing paler and more waxy with every moment. And the horrific, violent spurts—every pump of Ben's heart emptying him of blood—as the operating nurse placed her sterile, gloved hand over Pete's to take his place.

He'd been soaked with his lover's blood, dripping with it. He thought if he'd had to wait quietly until the surgery was over, he'd go crazy. He'd thrown himself back in the rescue effort, recklessly taking chances, until Irene had returned from helping a wounded soldier with the news that Ben was now in recovery. Once they were sure no one was left in the wreckage, he'd wanted to plant himself at Ben's bedside and never leave. It took Ginger's combined love and scolding to convince him he needed to wash up before he touched Ben.

Many of the nurses and doctors were wounded themselves, so the usual formal practices were modified as necessary, to account for missing crews. Strict military discipline was a bit lax.

Pete was allowed to stay at Ben's side—he didn't know why and he didn't really care. He suspected Ginger had a great deal to do with it. But, it didn't matter anymore—now that Ben was looking back at him with those blue eyes he'd dreamed of for so long.

Ben shook their joined hands gently, questioning.

"Sorry, um… distracted. Um, we need to keep you calm. If your blood pressure goes up, you could blow that patch-job right off. So, you need to stay calm. Okay, baby?"

"Okay." Ben's pulse had started hammering as soon as Pete mentioned it. He started to take deep breaths, trying to slow it.

"You were in the HQ when it was hit with a doodlebug—a robot bomb."

"I remember buzzing."

"That was it."

"And… and Gwen?"

Pete looked at him, sadly. "She didn't make it, baby."

Ben took in a sharp breath.

"Calm, baby, you gotta be calm."

It physically hurt to breathe. *Calm, Benjamin, calm. Calm down. Deep breaths. Come on now, Benjamin, deep breaths.*

"Her body took a great deal of the energy of the bomb blast, and a great deal of the shrapnel. She saved at least four soldiers, and you."

Tears slid down Ben's cheeks. *It hurts, calm, calm, calm, Benjamin, slow down.*

"The weight of her body on your leg is what kept you from bleeding to death before we could get you out."

"That's… if it had to happen, that's how she would have wanted to go… giving everything for… the soldiers."

Pete just nodded, tears in his eyes, squeezing Ben's hand tightly.

Ben squeezed his eyes shut against the tears, trying to match his breathing to Pete's.

CHAPTER FOURTEEN

THE DOCTORS INSISTED BEN NEEDED a bit more healing, longer periods of stable blood pressure, before they could fly him back to the States. He supervised, from his bed, the gathering of their props and costumes and the band's instruments to take inventory. The USO wanted to send them home as soon as possible—but the performers were adamant that they needed to finish the tour.

"You know as well as I do Gwen would have a fit—an absolute full-on screaming fit—if we left without seeing every soldier we could," Vicki fumed. "If we don't, she's going to come back from the grave and haunt us all."

Ben winced—maybe it was too soon to joke about Gwen's death? But no. No, that's exactly what she'd be doing if it were someone else dead. She looked life—or death—straight in the face and called a spade a spade.

Besides, she would. She'd be having a fit right now, screeching and probably throwing things and creating a ruckus and causing problems. Goddammit, he was going to miss her.

In the end, they salvaged enough costumes—and Ben modified a few things, hemming and mending in his hospital bed—and miraculously they had enough red lipstick and perfume to get them through the last two shows.

"You'd better make these the best two fucking shows you've ever done," Ben admonished, "or Gwen is really going to come back from the dead and steal all your clothes, and then you'll all have to go out there in nothing but your lipstick and perfume."

The crowd gathered around his bed chuckled sadly. The doctors wouldn't give him permission to go with them. Pete had looked as if he was about to sit on Ben's chest to hold him safe and sound in bed when Ben had complained.

* * *

BEN WAS RESTLESS, FRETTING AND impatient. He wanted to get out of bed, wanted to be free of needles and poking and bandages and pains. But he realized as soon as the doctors let him out of bed, they were going to ship him back to New York and he wouldn't see Pete again for God knows how long.

When Ginger was on duty, Pete was allowed to sit at Ben's bedside as long as he liked; Irene, too. Everyone seemed to have swallowed the story that Ben and Pete were cousins—childhood best friends. Charlie, when he came to visit, quipped, "If your mother is anything like my mother, Pete, she'll kill you with a spoon if you let anything happen to family."

Pete's crew had been stopping by to see Ben—even when Pete was not sitting next to him. Jim came one day, loping down the hall with his lanky cowboy swagger, a bunch of wildflowers in his hand.

"They grow along the airstrip. Somebody's going to go out and cut them all down soon, so I just thought… you might like them."

"Thank you, Jim. They're beautiful."

Jim dropped the rough bouquet in a cup of water standing on the table near Ben's bed.

"The rest of the crew and I… we… um. We're glad you're on the mend, Ben. We just want you to know that. We think the world of Pete, and… well. We sure are glad you're on the mend."

CHARLIE STOPPED BY, TOO, TOWING a shy and bashful Daisy along by the hand. Her dress was carefully pressed, her hair tamed into braids once again. She clutched Charlie's hand with both of hers, hiding behind him and peeping out with one eye.

"Aw, now you're gonna be shy?" Charlie cajoled. "You've been talking a mile a minute about wanting to come see Ben all day, and now you're not going to say anything to him?"

Pete slipped out of his chair and dropped to one knee in front of her. "Now, Daisy, I hear you helped get Ben back safe and sound and I'd like to thank you for helping him out."

She pressed her face into Charlie's side and giggled.

"Her mama asked me to bring her here to say thank you." Charlie smiled down at her.

"She's not a mama, she's a mum," Daisy explained earnestly. "And she said I must behave nicely and not be wild and not cause any ruckus."

"You're doing just fine, sweetheart," Ben murmured.

"Are you hurt very bad, Mr. Benjamin?" she asked.

"Nah," Ben wrinkled his nose and shook his head. "Not too badly, at least."

Pete scoffed at that, and was met by the most intense and grueling stare he's ever encountered, particularly from a nearly-six-year-old, judging him. She studied him for a long moment and apparently decided he was worthy. Abashed, he offered her his knee, and she primly clambered up, leaning forward to take Ben's hand. The rest of their afternoon was spent soaking up the small details, triumphs and trials of this small child, and Pete was thankful yet again for Ben's smile when their eyes met over her head.

* * *

A FEW DAYS LATER, BEN was finally pronounced "stable and ready for transport." A plane had flown over to fly him and the rest of the USO tour home.

Their final night together, Ben had to stay confined to his hospital bed, though Ginger was on duty and drew the curtain around it to give them some privacy. Ben grumbled, tried to plot a way to get out and go somewhere private where they could be alone together. But Pete would have none of it.

"They're not joking around, Ben. This is your life we're talking about."

"But..."

"No, Benjamin." Pete firmly took Ben's hand, looking seriously into his eyes. "I only just got you back. I'm not going to lose you again just for the sake of a little pleasure."

"Little? I'm hurt." Ben sniffed.

"Okay, massive, delectably lickable, huge, oh my God it's so big." Pete's eyes were wide as he played along.

Ben swatted at Pete's good arm. "You know it would be good."

"I do know it, baby," Pete whispered. "But, when I get home, we'll have all the time in the world. Once I get shipped home, and I get into our apartment, I never plan on leaving again."

"Oh, really?" Ben said, dryly.

"Really. I'm never leaving it again. Not to the market, not to the club, not to the office. I will become a recluse, and you will be my only link to civilization."

"Who said I'll be the link? What if I'm so sick of travel, *I* want to be the recluse."

"Too late," Pete said, airily. "I claimed it first."

Ben scoffed. "You fool."

"Yes, I will definitely become a recluse. Maybe even a hermit. I might even grow my beard out."

"Grow your beard out, and I'm never kissing you again. You know how sensitive my skin is to your whiskers."

"Well, then, absolutely no beard. Because never kissing you again? I'd waste away to nothing."

"You're giddy."

"I'm trying to be." Pete was suddenly serious.

"Why?"

"I can't come home with you." Pete sighed. "I finally asked about what's been holding up my discharge. Can't fly a plane with only one arm—or so I thought. Seems the powers-that-be think otherwise."

Ben grabbed Pete's hand, holding it fiercely.

"There's rumors... and whispers... something big is coming up. Soon. Some big airstrike, maybe or a battle planned, or—no one has any details, no one will commit to anything. But… they want me here for it. So, no medical discharge for me, like we thought."

Ben wanted to cry. He'd been—well, he'd never been convinced of it, but he'd been hoping and praying—that Pete's discharge would come through before his plane left the ground tomorrow. That they'd be able to fly back home together, hand-in-hand into the sunset, to leave all this behind them and live happily ever after.

But, of course not. Things like that only happened in fairy tales.

"Hey." Pete jiggled their linked hands. "Hey, don't look like that. We've still got tonight. And I'll be home soon."

"You better be. You promised."

"I still promise." Pete leaned forward and planted a kiss on the back of Ben's hand.

"I love you," Ben whispered.

"I love you, too."

* * *

WHEN THE PLANE TOOK OFF the next day, Ben had been loaded on a stretcher, the rest of the tour filing on solemnly behind him. Ginger was with him as his flight nurse. Her tour of duty was up, and her superiors were sending her home to rest before she'd be allowed to re-enlist. She'd become dangerously exhausted, they said, after running the hospital nearly by herself in the aftermath of the bombing, running double and triple shifts.

She argued vociferously, begged and pleaded: she wasn't any more exhausted than any of the other soldiers; she had to stay here and keep fighting for them, keep them safe and sound. Only Pete could convince her to go, as Ben's nurse.

"Please," Pete whispered into her hair as she cried into his arms. "I need him to live."

PETE STOOD ALONE ON THE airstrip, watching the plane carrying his love taxi slowly down the runway.

He wasn't really alone—the crew of the Riveting Redhead stood just behind him. Irene was there, too, and Reggie from the auto-pool, and Emily from the mess hall and everyone who's come to care so deeply for this man who'd been so kind and gracious and helpful and sweet to them— they were all behind him, waiting to help him with whatever he needed.

Pete was successful in keeping his tears at bay, there on the tarmac. With a kind smile, he greeted everyone who stopped to say a kind word to him.

Jim and Bill and Charlie came up, last. No one said much of anything, though Charlie's eyes were a bit red and Bill sniffled.

"Buy you a beer, Cap'n?" Jim asked.

"Thanks. Yeah." Pete nodded, sniffing.

Charlie threw an arm around Pete's neck as Jim clapped him on his good shoulder. Ben may be gone—headed back to safety and hot showers and good food and home—but Pete still had his crew.

* * *

THE PRESS HAD A FIELD day with Gwen's death and funeral—spinning it into propaganda as only the War Department could allow them to do— *patriotic girl makes the ultimate sacrifice while doing her patriotic duty.* Pete was disgusted by it.

They'd taken a photo of Ben, tall and slim and grave, leaning heavily on a cane as he walked, all alone, into the church.

Pete's heart hurt to see the photos in the paper, even knowing that Bets had been there, somewhere. But Ben looked so... so aloof and distant and alone. Pete's fingers ached to reach out and smooth Ben's lapel, though surely it had been tailored so perfectly there would be no need for adjustments; to gently brush Ben's hair off his forehead; to take his arm, ostensibly to help him walk, and squeeze his bicep, hard—anything to let Ben know he was not alone.

Pete neatly tore the photo of Ben from the paper—everyone else in the mess hall had read it by now—and slipped it in his pocket. He finished his coffee, deftly stacked his dishes on his tray and swept it up with one hand. He was getting better at it. Thank God it was his left shoulder, not his right, but going through life with one arm strapped to his body was going to drive him insane. He couldn't wait for it to heal so he could get rid of these restrictive bandages.

He slowly walked back to his barracks, tripping on the doorframe on his way in, as usual. He sat heavily on his bunk; its springs squeaked loudly. Setting his tongue between his teeth, he pulled with his one good arm and pushed with his feet and managed to drag his heavy footlocker within reach.

Inside Pete's footlocker, everything was neat and tidy. The top tray held his six pairs of standard Army issue wool socks—dark green, and two pairs of dark brown gloriously thick and warm wool socks his mother had knit him. Various rank insignia, a pair of cuff links, a button he had to sew back on his overcoat and an obnoxiously patterned, brightly colored bow tie Bets sent him for his birthday.

Below the tray were his neatly folded uniforms, a few novels Ben had sent him, a small box filled with neatly stacked letters from home and a small leather-bound photo album almost full with snapshots—the people in them varying, but nearly always a tall young man with laughing eyes and a wide smile was somewhere in the crowd. In the cardboard box nestled in the middle, he'd stashed little trinkets and doo-dads he'd picked up along the way. He'd sent them home packed in Ben's bag.

It was cold. It was always cold in their barracks, but now the wind whistled through the window frames as if the glass wasn't even there. He clicked on the overhead light, just a bulb hanging from its wire in the center of the room, and drew the blackout curtains to try to block the draft and cut out the weak late-morning light. The rest of his crew was off somewhere—helping out, filling in where they could, doing whatever needed to be done. He was on strict orders to rest—the last time they'd re-strapped his arm, the doctor swore if he saw Pete doing something that might reinjure his shoulder, he'd confine him to a hospital bed.

Pete awkwardly pulled out the tray of his footlocker, fumbled for the photo album and a book and replaced the tray. He let the lid of the locker slam down and carefully laid down on his bed. He'd found that flopping on his bed, as he used to, was jarring to his damn shoulder.

He flipped through the photos—he'd slipped the photos from Glenn's journal inside, and he took a moment to remember his friend as he looked at them. The next photo was Ben and Bets and Ginger and Tony and Pete sitting around a dining table, beaming at the camera. There was Pete, laughing at Bets holding his birthday cake covered in candles in front of him, Ben to one side of him, smiling fondly. A photo of the day they'd all gone to the Statue of Liberty and Bets and Ginger got blisters from their new shoes and begged him and Ben for piggyback rides. They'd asked a stranger to take their photo; Ginger nearly tipped Ben over with her excitement; Bets looked cute as all hell as she clung to Pete's back.

Two of his favorites weren't of people at all. In one, he'd tried to take a picture for his mother of the painting they'd just hung in their dining room—a painting that had been his grandmother's. It was perfectly balanced between two gorgeous candelabras they'd found buried at a flea market. He had set up the shot perfectly. Then Ben, not knowing Pete was taking a photo, walked through the corner of the shot. People who didn't know what they were looking at just saw a grayish smear at the side of the photo, but Pete could see the outline of Ben's broad shoulders and his hair in an unruly just-out-of-bed coif.

The other, also originally to be sent to his mother, showed the view out their living room window: a somewhat boring landscape shot, unless someone noticed in the corner of the photo the hand holding back the curtains. The trees and the small park beyond were somewhat blurry, but the hand was in sharp focus, the delicate veins crisscrossing the back of it, the long, lean fingers, the strength in them apparent. Ben's hand.

Pete slipped the newsprint photo into the photo album and sighed. He put his good arm behind his head, and thought he'd try to read, but fell asleep instead, the photo album balanced securely over his heart.

* * *

SEVERAL DAYS AFTER THE FUNERAL, there was an all-star Hollywood memorial tribute to the late, great Gwen Andrews. It was tasteful—classy, even. Pete, listening to it on the radio in the nearly empty officer's club with Jim, Bill and Charlie, was certain that wherever Gwen Andrews was now, she was undoubtedly rolling her eyes and throwing up her hands. Classy and tasteful were two things Gwen had always aspired never to be.

Pete leaned back in his chair, hissing in pain as he bumped his shoulder.

"Mama said it's the best pain relief," Charlie said cheerfully, as he set another glass of whiskey down in front of Pete.

Pete smiled—Charlie's mama knew best after all, and took a large slug of it.

"And finally," the radio announcer's voice boomed, "we have a very dear friend of Miss Andrews. Ladies and gentleman, please welcome Benjamin Williams to the stage."

The applause was thunderous. Pete's head buzzed with excitement, the anticipation of hearing Ben's voice again mixing with the whiskey he'd been drinking.

Faintly came the gentle clearing of Ben's throat—and Pete thrilled that he could recognize Ben even from that small sound.

"Thank you." Ben's voice was warm. "Tonight, I'd like to sing for you two of Gwen's favorite songs. And I'd like to say 'Gwen, honey, this is for you.' But I know what she'd say to that. 'No way, sugarcakes.'"

The audience laughed.

"So instead, I'd like to dedicate these songs to our men and women in uniform. Gwen's life, these past few years, was all for you. Every song she sang, every picture she took, every word she said—was all with you in mind. She wanted to make your lives a little happier, a little sunnier, even if just for a minute. She died as she would have wanted—saving soldiers' lives."

Ben sucked in a shaking breath. Pete instinctively leaned forward toward the radio, toward him.

"I knew her well enough to know she'd say her only regret is that she couldn't save more of you."

He paused again, steadying his voice.

"And now, without further ado, these next songs are dedicated to Our Boys Over There."

Pete instinctively closed his eyes as Ben began to sing "P.S. I Love You"—a seemingly silly little song of loved ones being apart and writing each other of their mundane everyday lives, but always underscoring everything with the reassurance of enduring love and faithfulness. Pete didn't doubt that it was one of Gwen's favorites—it would have showcased her voice perfectly—but he knew Ben was singing to him, for him, tonight.

The audience applauded loudly and Pete realized the boys at the table with him had joined in it. He opened his eyes, smiled and took a drink. He thought he might have had more whiskey than he realized, but he didn't care.

Ben didn't speak between songs; the orchestra segued between them. His voice was low, with a breathless throatiness Pete hadn't heard before. Pete's eyes closed again so he could picture Ben—Ben undoubtedly keeping time with the swaying of his hips, rocking them gently in time to the music.

Ben's voice was caressing, lovingly embracing each note, each word. Pete felt them, felt them as if Ben were singing them into his skin as kisses. Ben's voice soaring, then dropping to his lower register gave Pete goose bumps. He shivered with want, with the need for Ben in his arms, to be in Ben's arms.

As Ben's voice faded away and the radio program ended, Pete realized the officer's club had gone silent. Opening his eyes, he was relieved to see only Jim, Charlie and Bill remained. He didn't realize he'd been crying until Jim nudged his good arm, silently handing him a handkerchief.

Charlie, his eyes warm and caring, gave him a sympathetic smile. "'Nother whiskey, Cap'n?"

Pete nodded gratefully. He didn't know how, or for how long, but these boys—his friends, his comrades—seemed to *know* about him and Ben and it didn't seem to matter at all. He was profoundly relieved and thankful.

"Gosh, did you hear the trade Red Sox made yesterday?" Bill snapped off the radio, changing the subject.

"Don't you start in on the Sox, boy," Charlie warned. Jim shouted with laughter—this was one of their regular arguments and it always ended outrageously.

Sometimes Pete really loved these boys.

CHAPTER FIFTEEN

Time passed. Seasons changed. Ben still volunteered at the USO canteen, and had taken an extra job at a parachute factory outside the city. Despite it being winter, he began to spend most of his time at the beach house, far from loud noises that still made him jump and flashing lights that caused him to break out in a panic. It was quiet and peaceful out there. He wrote Pete daily, occasionally wrote to other members of Pete's crew. He sent letters and packages to Ginger, who was now away teaching at the nursing school where she'd graduated.

Pete's shoulder healed enough to return to duty. He wrote Ben every day, even when there was nothing much to tell him, beyond that he loved him, that he was safe and he was coming home to him.

* * *

The crew of the Riveting Redhead was two flights away from their quota—every bomber crew was required to run twenty-five flights, and then they'd be sent home. So far, only one crew had actually made to the quota. The rest had all been lost.

Their second-to-last run felt routine, by now. Flak, shrapnel, enemy fighters, cloud cover, desperately cold temperatures, smoke screens covering the target—they were used to it.

The real excitement didn't come until they got close to base—damage to the plane's underside meant the landing gear wouldn't extend. Pete would have to glide the plane down on its belly or risk driving it straight into the ground.

As they got closer, the crew fell silent. They were almost always nearly out of fuel by the time they returned, but they circled several times to ensure they had the least possible amount of flammable liquid onboard. Other planes landed and quickly taxied out of their way.

On his final approach, Pete could see the emergency trucks already lining the landing strip. *Just concentrate and land, Montgomery. It's not that much different from a regular landing.* His hands were steady as he guided the plane toward the rapidly approaching earth.

It wasn't perfect. They still slammed hard enough to knock everything about. As they barreled along the ground, ripping up grass and shrubs and dirt in their wake, the plane snapped and popped, a propeller catching and groaning as it twisted. He had little to no control over the plane now they were on the ground, having to rely on friction to slow the frenzied slide of the massive aircraft to a halt. He gripped the stick tightly, regardless of its futility, and felt a sharp pop in his shoulder. He heard another pop, and gasped as his vision went momentarily white.

The plane finally skidded to a stop. They all scrambled to vault from the plane. Pete fell to the ground, Jim picking him up by the waist and all but carrying him away from the plane that ticked and hissed and popped menacingly. When they finally stopped, far enough to be safely away from any explosions from the plane, Pete fell to his knees and vomited—his shoulder was out of joint again and the pain finally hit him.

But then, Charlie was on his knees right beside him, puking his own guts out, and he wasn't even injured. Charlie grinned sheepishly at him when he was finished, wiping his mouth.

"Bill? Looks like we gotta get Cap'n to the doc. Again."

THEY DID EVERYTHING THEY COULD to put Pete's shoulder back in its socket. It just wouldn't stay.

When he woke a few mornings later, in his own bed, groggy from painkillers and more sore than he'd ever been in his life, there was his crew standing around him.

"I'm so sorry, guys." Pete didn't think he'd ever felt so guilty in his life—and angry, too. They were all so close to going home and now his fucking shoulder meant they couldn't make that last flight, so they were all stuck here a little longer, waiting for him to hurry up and fucking heal already.

"Cap'n." Charlie looked surprisingly cheerful. "Get your bags packed. You're going home."

Pete was stunned.

"Home? But…"

"No buts, Montgomery," Bill said, his voice firm. "Get your ass out of bed, on the double. Your flight leaves in an hour."

"An hour?" Pete sat up so quickly he was dizzy.

"Well, to be honest, you don't need to pack." Jim gestured to a large rucksack on the floor beside him. "We packed everything for you already."

"You packed…"

"Montgomery!" Their commanding officer barged through the door. Pete tried to stand at attention as fast he could, but Bill pushed him back down to sit on the bed.

"At ease, soldier," The C.O. barked, nodding sharply at all of them. "Good, I see you're all packed. Here are your official orders. Your discharge paperwork should come in the mail in a few weeks. Until then, consider yourself home on leave. Report to the VA hospital indicated in the paperwork as soon as you can for surgery on your shoulder and rehabilitation. There's one stop we'd like to you make on your way—the information is all in the envelope."

Pete took the stack of paperwork with his good arm. He didn't believe this was happening.

"But, sir… what about… what about my men? My crew?"

The C.O. smiled slightly. "Do you think I'm about to hand this crew *another* plane? You've lost two now, and with only one flight left in your quota—and in light of everything you've all done here above and beyond your duties—we're going to send them home, too, on a later flight. These boys will make fine instructors at any flight school they choose."

"Thank you… Thank you, sir," Pete stammered.

"Now, the first available flight is in," he said, checking his watch, "thirty-nine minutes. I expect you on it, Captain."

"Yes sir. Yes, I will be."

The C.O. softened, smiling wider at him. "I'm sorry for the rush, Montgomery. Is there anyone back home we could send a telegram to, so they'd know to come pick you up?

"No, sir. I'd like—I'd like it to be a surprise."

"Good. Now, get on that plane, Captain."

A FEW MINUTES LATER, PETE hurried toward the flight line, Jim carrying his rucksack for him, the rest of his entire crew following behind him. They all but shoved him on the plane, promising to send his love and best wishes to everyone he wanted to say goodbye to: *Montgomery just sit down in the fucking plane, we won't forget to tell Irene goodbye for you.*

Charlie helped him buckle his seat belt, settling it more comfortably across his shoulder, winking at the flight nurse standing nearby.

He smiled brightly at Pete, shaking his good hand. "Now, you tell your cousin Ben that we all send him our best."

Pete pulled him down to his seat for a hug. "And," Charlie continued in a whisper, "if you don't give him the biggest fucking kiss you've ever given him when you first see him, me and the boys have agreed that we're coming to kick your ass, just so you're aware."

Pete gasped out a laugh and nodded. Bill and Jim gave him quick hugs, then were shooed off the plane by the flight nurse. The hatch had barely closed before the plane started to taxi. Pete looked out the window and saw them all—more people than he'd realized had come out to see him off—waving frantically and smiling for all they were worth.

This was it. Pete Montgomery was on his way home.

CHAPTER SIXTEEN

THE MORNING BEFORE PETE'S BIRTHDAY dawned hot and humid. Even in the early morning with the sun bright on the horizon, the heat rose off the beach. Pete lay in the hammock stretched between two scrub pines, swinging listlessly, as Ben puttered in the kitchen.

They'd been staying out at the bungalow since the weather turned warm—swimming was good exercise for his shoulder and while he stubbornly swam every single morning, he'd spent the rest of the day in the hammock. It had been a long time—far too long, in his opinion, since he'd been able to do much of anything without his goddamned shoulder giving him grief. He kept one leg over the side, stretching out to push his toe against the dirt to keep himself swinging.

"Darling?" Ben called through the kitchen window. "Would you like anything to drink?"

"No." Pete had to clear his throat. "No, thank you. I'm fine."

"Ready for breakfast?"

"Not hungry, thanks."

Ben tried to be supportive, tried to be loving and take care of Pete, even when he didn't want to be taken care of. It had been six months since Pete came home, six months of being together again, and while Pete had been exuberant at first, the very real on-going limitations of his injury had been weighing heavily on him. What hurt Ben the worst was that the blazing light that always seemed to be pouring out of Pete, the glow of his skin, the sparkle of his eyes, were dimmed and dull.

A slamming of car doors, and Bets breezed into the kitchen, her tiny arms full of grocery bags.

"How is he?" she asked, nodding out the window towards the tousled hair just visible over the edge of the hammock.

"About the same. God, I hope this is right."

"It'll be good for him."

"God, I hope so." Ben began to put groceries away, stashing extra beer in the icebox.

PETE'S EYES WERE CLOSED, BUT he could hear someone walking gently through the grass toward him. It was probably Ben. He sighed and tried to rouse himself to take an interest in whatever Ben was going to say. It pained him that he had to actively think about being interested in Ben right now—a sharp pain somewhere near his heart. *Am I dying?* He just found it so hard to take an interest in things these days, as if everything he did was a struggle, a weight, dragging him down. He'd spent so long under such constant stress, piloting the Redhead through such dangerous conditions, that he had a hard time remembering what it was like to live everyday civilian life. He was waiting, every day, for *something*, but he didn't know what he was waiting *for.* He was stuck in a quagmire, not quite able to settle back into regular life. He had lived so long with death and danger always on the horizon, and now he lived in a cold dreading numbness that it would come back.

A cold bottle, slick with condensation, was pressed into his hand.

"Jesus, Cap'n. You look like shit."

Pete's eyes flew open and he fumbled out of the hammock before he quite knew what he was doing. He launched himself at Charlie—his crewman, his comrade, his friend.

Charlie was tall enough that Pete didn't knock him over, but he stumbled a bit as he caught Pete in a hug.

"Hey! You're gonna spill my beer!" Charlie didn't really sound like he minded.

"What the hell are you doing here, Charlie?" Pete clapped him on the shoulder.

"I heard you were having a birthday or something."

From the kitchen, Ben could see Pete's grin—the grin he hadn't seen in months, and his heart soared at the sight of it.

"Hey, someone said there was going to be beer here," Jim drawled as he came around the corner of the house, wearing a ridiculous straw cowboy hat and the ugliest shirt Ben had ever seen.

"What the hell are you both doing here?" Pete's head swiveled between the two of them, beaming.

"Benjamin said you—"

"Wait, Ben called you?"

"The man sent me homemade lemon pound cake overseas. Twice. They were even better than my grandma's." Charlie took a long drink of his beer, shrugging. "I owe him one."

Pete laughed, for what seemed like the first time in weeks.

"Pretty nice place you got here, Pete." Jim was standing, one hand on his hip, surveying their tiny cottage. "Nice view, too." He gestured with his beer bottle at the expanse of ocean beyond, behind the rose bushes, their lawn melting out into the beach sand.

"Yeah, thanks. We like it." Pete shielded his eyes from the bright sunlight with his hand.

"Is this where the party is?" Bill was suddenly standing at the backyard gate.

"Bill!" Pete hurried to open the gate for him.

"And I knew it'd be crap beer. Brought my own," he said tersely, hauling a cooler behind him.

"Holy shit." Pete's grin was so wide it looked as though his face should hurt. "Benny! Benjamin, get out here!"

Ben eventually emerged from the back door, smiling shyly, carrying a large tray of food. Bets followed with a tray of glasses and ice. Ginger sauntered out, carrying nothing at all.

"How did you... when did... how long can you all stay for?" Pete stumbled over his words in his excitement.

"I'm here for at least a week." Charlie stretched himself out in the hammock, curling his arms behind his head. "Maybe even longer."

Ginger bumped the hammock with her hip, causing him to flail to stay in it.

"Everyone else is headed out tomorrow, I think." Bill settled himself on the grass, passing a bottle of beer to Jim, who opened it on the edge of the picnic table.

"Tony said to say sorry he's not here. But his mother wouldn't let him come." Even Jim cracked a smile as the rest of them howled with laughter. Tony'd always been a mama's boy.

"And the other guys sent their apologies for not being able to get here, too."

"It's just so good to see you guys." The warmth and life in Pete's eyes made Ben's eyes prick with tears.

"Cap'n, you need to drink your beer while it's still cold," Charlie instructed. "Or are you feeling homesick for England?"

They all laughed. His crew was rumpled and sun-bleached in their civilian clothes, tanned, relaxed and happy in a way Pete had never seen them. He punched Charlie's arm playfully, took a huge swig of his beer and winked at Ben, who beamed nearby.

Lunch had been forgotten in the excitement of seeing everyone again, and they'd moved to the beach for dinner—roasting hot dogs over the campfire Bill built. Everyone was stuffed full, sprawled out on the blankets covering the sand. The beer had been flowing all day, along with whiskey sours and Manhattans when Bets could be coaxed to go back to the house to mix them up. Everyone was giggling and tipsy, in that wonderful summer-night-time way when the only worry was finding a comfortable place to sleep, no responsibilities, nothing to anticipate but the next laugh from your friends; and Pete was fairly sure he was definitely actually drunk. Definitely.

"Thank you, sugar," Jim slurred, as Bets handed him another drink. She giggled flirtatiously, stumbling a little on the sand, and not-so-accidentally falling to the sand right next to him. He flung his arm around her shoulder as she whispered something in his ear.

Pete wondered if he should say something to her—or to him. But, they we're both good people and Bets was a big girl who could take care of herself. And besides, Ben was warm at his side, leaning against him. Without the sun, the air was suddenly chilly around him.

"Hey!" Charlie called from where he lay on his back, staring at the sky.

Jim and Bets were still canoodling. Tommy and Bill made Ginger laugh at something, probably more dirty jokes. Ben sat beside him, humming softly under his breath, his legs tucked up tightly to his chest, tracing patterns in the sand near their feet.

Pete was mesmerized by it, couldn't stop watching his beautiful hands— God those hands can do so much—tracing. In a few moments, he realized Ben was tracing "I love you" over and over in the sand. He nudged him with his good shoulder. Ben nudged him back, looking up at him through those impossibly long eyelashes. Pete was just about to lean down and whisper something into his ear, something dirty, something hot, something wanting, when he realized Charlie was sliding himself over to them through the sand. He stopped abruptly next to Pete, drunk, off-balance and bleary.

"So, did you?" he hissed loudly.

"I have no idea what you're talking about, Thompson. What the hell are you talking about?" Pete was careful in his enunciation, knowing he wasn't really that drunk. Not really. Well, maybe a little bit that drunk. He giggled.

"I told you when I last saw you that you'd better give him the biggest kiss you've ever given him when you first saw him or we'd have to come and kick your ass, and I just want to know if you did or not," Charlie whispered as if this was the most reasonable thing ever.

Pete just smiled.

Christmas day, Pete had finally came home. The snow had crunched lightly under the tires as the taxi pulled away from the beach house. It was early morning, barely light and the cabbie had insisted on carrying his bag right to his front door, had wanted to wait until Pete had unlocked it to carry them inside. But Pete had explained he was trying to surprise someone, and he just needed to be alone to do it. The cabbie had winked, and driven away.

He'd unlocked the door with the key under the mat, wincing at noise as the bolt slid back. He'd opened the door carefully, dragged his bag inside—he still couldn't lift much of anything with his damn shoulder—and gently eased it closed behind him.

Pete's eyes had welled with tears when he saw Ben's Christmas decorations, just the same as every year. He'd known it was Christmas, but it had never felt like Christmas without Ben. He'd reported to Armed Forces Radio and they'd recorded him singing that song—that song for Ben, that always made him think of Ben and of sitting here with him in front of the fire. He hoped Ben had heard it.

His chair had been drawn up to the fireplace, close to Ben's. Ben had hung the mistletoe, just as he always did, on the arm of his reading lamp, so it hung close to his head whenever he sat there. *Not that I need any excuse to kiss you,* Ben had always archly said.

He slipped off his coat, gasping as the movement jarred his shoulder—at least the strapping was off for now—slipped off his boots and gingerly climbed the stairs, avoiding the second-to-last one that always popped when he stepped on it.

He crept down the hall to their room, the door left open to catch any warmth from the fireplace. Ben was in Pete's pajamas, lying on sheets so blue they matched his eyes. Or, they would match them, once his eyes were open.

Pete stripped off his clothes—he couldn't believe Ben hadn't woken up yet. He grabbed the edge of the quilts, slid into bed next to Ben, next to his lover, and laid his head on his old pillow.

Pete grinned as Ben opened his eyes sleepily.

"Hi baby." Ben voice was rough, his eyes still blinking drowsily. He reached out to trace Pete's lips with one fingertip. "I love you. You're so beautiful. I love you. I have so many things I want to tell you, baby, but I can't remember them all while I'm sleeping. This is such a good dream, baby, I don't want it to end. You look so real. You feel so real. I don't want this dream to end. Can you stay longer this time, baby?"

"I'll stay forever." Pete brushed Ben's hair off his forehead with one hand, still smiling. He'd always loved Ben's habit of sleep talking. "But it's not a dream, baby. It's not. I'm here. I'm here, and I'm not going away again. I'm home."

"You always say that. In these dreams." Ben's eyes blinked closed again. "I always believe you. But you always say that, and then I wake up and I'm alone again."

"Then I'll stay until you wake up again. But, first, darling, roll over. I want to hold you."

Ben rolled to his other side, facing away from Pete, already nearly asleep again. Pete slid one arm under his neck, wrapped his other arm around Ben's waist and pulled him close. He twined their fingers, pressing their clasped hands against Ben's heart.

"This is all I've been wanting. All I've been needing," Pete whispered in Ben's ear. "Just you."

"S'good dream." Ben mumbled. "So real. You're so real. So beautiful. So warm. Your body. So warm. Always so warm, except your feet. I never understand why your feet are so cold."

Ben's eyes snapped open in surprise and he shrieked as Pete's cold toes found Ben's warm feet. "Oh my God! Your toes are so goddamned cold, what are you doing to me? Why are you doing this—this is not how this dream goes. You're supposed to start kissing the back of my neck and then we have sex. You don't come in here and freeze my goddamned legs off with your goddamned icicle toes!"

Pete convulsed with laughter behind Ben, his arms tightening around his lover so tightly that Ben couldn't turn his body, only his head, as he turned to see—really see—Pete. His eyes filled with tears.

"Oh my God. It's not a dream. It's really you. You're really here."

"I'm really here, baby. I'm home."

Pete relaxed his arms, just enough for Ben to turn over, both of them reaching out to touch the face of the other, wiping away each other's tears.

"My shoulder's been refusing to stay in the socket, after that last hard landing we did. And the Air Forces won't let you fly a bomber without both arms fully functioning. They discharged me. I wanted to surprise you, so I didn't send a telegram."

Ben's mouth worked soundlessly. The tears started again, for both of them.

Pete reached down, pressed a fervent kiss to his love's lips. "I'm home, Ben, and I'm never leaving you again."

No, HE HADN'T GIVEN HIM the biggest kiss when he'd *first* seen him; there had been Ben's dreaming and Pete's cold toes to contend with. But, after all that had been squared away, there had been kissing, and since, for the rest of the day and most of the day after, Pete's mouth hadn't really left Ben's body, he supposed that could count as the biggest kiss he'd ever given him.

But Pete's pretty sure Charlie's not ready to hear about that.

"He most certainly did," Ben boldly answered Charlie's question, brushing beach sand off Pete's bare foot familiarly.

"Good," Charlie said emphatically. "I just wanted to be sure."

He stood abruptly, without saying more, and lurched off towards the beer cooler.

Ben turned to him. Pete thought he was probably blushing, but couldn't tell in the moonlight. What he could tell was that the moon was making his skin glow. Ben always talked about Pete's skin glowing in the sunlight, but Ben glowed in the moonlight, like marble, like a thing of impossible beauty, and Pete reached out and put his hand, unsteadily, on Ben's cheek to remind himself again that he was real. Ben was real and Pete was here and neither of them would ever have to be apart from the other ever again. This was real.

Pete started to giggle before his lips had even left Ben's. Ben's eyes were full of love and moonlight and Pete couldn't resist kissing him again, Ben's mouth opening under his and *oh God, this is going to be too much for everyone else, but oh God I'm not stopping now.*

When the realization dawned that there are no whoops or hollers, catcalls or wolf-whistles from anyone else, Ben drew back slightly. Pete still held Ben's face, lovingly, and they kept their foreheads nearly pressed together as they rolled their heads inquisitively to the side.

Bill's elbow had collapsed under him, passed out on the sand. He was snoring loudly.

Jim was sprawled at the edge of the firelight, Bets' small body in her white sundress on top of him, pushing him flat.

All they could see of Charlie was his bare feet—his very large, bare feet, which were flailing in surprise. They heard Ginger, unsuccessfully trying to keep her voice quiet, hissing, "Dammit, Charlie. I've been waiting for months for you to do it on your own, and you just haven't, so will you just fucking kiss me already?"

"I… you… just… sure!" Charlie stammered.

And then everything was quiet.

Ben started to giggle. Pete started to giggle.

"Oh my God."

"No one's going to notice a thing now," Pete teased in Ben's ear, sliding his hands down to the waist of Ben's shorts.

"Peter Montgomery. There is absolutely no way we are having sex right here in front of our friends, no matter how preoccupied they might be."

"Oh," Pete wheedled, kissing Ben's neck, "no sex. Just a little fun."

"Fun, you can have. Sex, too, if you'll help me find my way back to our bedroom. But you forget how *irritating* sand can be."

Pete remembered. Oh, how Pete remembered. That had not been a good night. Or a good rest of the week, really.

They stood, pulling each other up, giggling at how unsteady they were.

"Oh, look at the time," Pete said loudly, to no one in particular. "I'll think we'll say goodnight now."

No one seemed to have heard, though Pete thought he might have seen Charlie weakly wave them away.

Pete and Ben wove their way back to the house, climbed the stairs on hands and knees, kissing and giggling all the way. The rest of their night was full of lazy kisses and caressing and Ben holding Pete so tight neither of them could breathe, but neither of them cared.

* * *

IN THE MORNING, WHEN THEY came downstairs, they found Bill fast asleep on the couch. Jim and Bets slept curled up on the living room carpet, her head pillowed on his chest.

A little while later, as the four of them made breakfast, Charlie and Ginger came in from the beach. Ginger, her hair wild and tousled, was wearing Charlie's jacket.

They ate breakfast, the seven of them, laughing sheepishly, giggling and making plans to rent boats for Pete's birthday and coming back here to spend Christmas. Jim announced he wanted to have *his* birthday here as well. Charlie announced that he was moving in. The walls of the tiny house rocked with laughter.

Ben took Pete's hand and pressed a kiss to it. Pete smiled, his heart in his eyes. He was full of light and lightness. No more waiting, ever again, for either of them. Their life, together again, began now.

THE END

ACKNOWLEDGMENTS

THIS BOOK WOULD NEVER HAVE seen the light of day without the host of people behind me, to whom many thanks and more are due:

First, to my boys for being the breath to my life and my joy's light. You are the love of my life and I am thankful for you, every single day. Ever yours, ever mine, ever ours.

To my team at Interlude Press, for their belief in me, and their encouragement, tenacity and style. Also for how hard you guys make me laugh.

To my editor, Annie, for having the kindest heart and the toughest red pencil. You've helped me make so many of my dreams come true. Thank you for always having my back.

To Lex for his invaluable help with everything from corrupted files to random trivia about the Andrews Sisters. Thank you a million times over.

To Mims, Brew, and especially to Axe – for ridiculous amounts of laughter, honesty, sass and love. This story never would have made it off the ground without you. I call dibs on being your Rose.

To Ginny, for being the first person to ever hear this story as I babbled it out on our trips to the park, and Ginny-and-Matti, both, for champagne, loving friendship and "angry villagers." You guys mean the world to me.

To Jimmy and the Yankees Fan – for good things coming out of strange situations, talking me out of the corners I'd thought myself into and never ever failing to answer my "pop quiz, hot shot" queries, no matter how random.

To The Girls: Reia, Nicole, Ginny, and Brenda, for wild karaoke nights, good advice and cafe visits whenever I needed them.

To my dad, my siblings and the rest of my family for love, laughter and truly fabulous music.

Special thanks and love to folks who keep me going on a daily basis—Carrie, Lissa, Katrina, my Kitchen, Pet, Darren, Lynn, Claire, Jude, Chris, Olive, B, L, Sam, Jo, Lindsey, the other Sam, Batty & Bella, my Izmeister, Colleen, Patsy, Leah, Becca, Courtney, Katelyn, Mes Parisiennes, and my beloved Pantsters.

And to everyone who sent me encouragement during the writing of this book – I've appreciated and treasured every single word.

ABOUT THE AUTHOR

K.E. BELLEDONNE IS A WRITER, editor and translator based in the French Alps. A native New Englander, Kat enjoys good food and good wine, listening to Glenn Miller and Artie Shaw records, and cheering on her beloved Red Sox. *Right Here Waiting* is her first novel. Her second novel, *Daniel & Erik's Super Fab Ultimate Wedding Checklist*, was published in 2016.

interludepress.com
@InterludePress
interludepress
store.interludepress.com

interlude press™
you may also like...

Daniel & Erik's Super Fab Ultimate Wedding Checklist by K.E. Belledonne

When Daniel gets caught up in the demands of a cheeky wedding planning app, his fiancé Erik grows frustrated with his preoccupation with adhering to heterosexual traditions. Will Daniel's groomzilla ways give them the wedding of their dreams, or ultimately lead to their relationship's demise?

ISBN (print) 978-1-941530-82-5 | (eBook) 978-1-941530-83-2

Bitter Springs by Laura Stone

In 1870s Texas, the youngest son of a large, traditional family has been sent to train with a freed slave and talented mesteñero so he can continue the family horse trade. *Bitter Springs* tells the story of a man coming into his own and realizing his destiny lies in the wild open spaces with a man who loves him, far from expectations of society.

ISBN (print) 978-1-941530-55-9 | (eBook) 978-1-941530-56-6

Speakeasy by Suzey Ingold

In the height of the Prohibition era in Manhattan, recent Yale graduate Heath Johnson falls for Art, the proprietor of a unique speakeasy where men are free to explore their sexuality. When Art's sanctuary is raided, Heath is forced to choose between love and the structured life his parents planned for him.

ISBN (print) 978-1-941530-69-6 | (eBook) 978-1-941530-70-2